MW00760471

About the Author

Dean lives in Arizona with his wife Sherry and their Pomeranian dog Floyd. His hobbies include exploring the desert, target shooting, and reading.
Gone and Forgotten is his first novel.

Dedication

This book is dedicated to the four women in my life: my wife, my mother, my daughter, and my sister.

I would also like to thank the people who helped me complete the novel by reading sections and providing feedback or by simply providing support. These people include my wife Sherry, my mother Thelma, and my friends Larry aka "Wyatt", Linda aka "Mrs. Mayweather", and Forrest aka "Matt".

Lastly, I would like to thank both my parents and my grandparents for instilling in me not only an appreciation of historical events but also a curiosity of why events and things happened the way they did.

F. Dean Pulley

GONE AND FORGOTTEN

Thank you for reading my book!

Dn Pulley

AUSTIN MACAULEY
PUBLISHERS LTD.

Copyright © F. Dean Pulley (2015)

The right of F. Dean Pulley to be identified as author of this work has been asserted by him in accordance with section 77 and 78 of the Copyright, Designs and Patents Act 1988.

All rights reserved. No part of this publication may be reproduced, stored in a retrieval system, or transmitted in any form or by any means, electronic, mechanical, photocopying, recording, or otherwise, without the prior permission of the publishers.

Any person who commits any unauthorized act in relation to this publication may be liable to criminal prosecution and civil claims for damages.

A CIP catalogue record for this title is available from the British Library.

ISBN 978 1 78455 233 6 (Paperback)
ISBN 978 1 78455 235 0 (Hardback)

www.austinmacauley.com

First Published (2015)
Austin Macauley Publishers Ltd.
25 Canada Square
Canary Wharf
London
E14 5LB

Printed and bound in Great Britain

Introduction

My name is Henry. However, most people call me Hank. People call me Hank because Hank was my father's nickname, and in my small town it was a necessary obligation that the son be given the same nickname as the father. The fact that his real name was also Henry, and that I was named after him, made this nickname obligation a requirement. Looking back, I realize that no one ever asked me what name I preferred. If anyone had asked, then I would have told them that I would have preferred to be called Doc.

Growing up in my small town had advantages and it also had a couple of distinct disadvantages. I don't like to make generalizations, but I think it is safe to assume that some of these disadvantages are true for all small towns. One disadvantage is that everyone knew everyone and it had been that way for generations. As a young boy, hardly a day would pass that I did not encounter some older person who had a story to tell about his father and my grandfather, and sometimes he could even tell a story about our great grandfathers. As a result, there were few family secrets. In fact, I would say that there were no family secrets. There were only family things that were talked about and family things that were never talked about. Because there were really no secrets, there were self-proclaimed experts on the personal business of everyone else. My father called these people busybodies. It was funny to watch one of these busy bodies encounter another townsperson on the sidewalk. The busybody did not really need to ask what the other person had been up to because the busybody already knew what the person had been up to, but the busybody would always ask if for no other reason than to confirm their own sense of self importance.

There is one thing that I think would be a safe generalization to make about small towns, which is that people don't forget what happens in a small town.

The second disadvantage of growing up in my small town was that being different meant being noticed. The population of the town was small so it was almost impossible not to get noticed for something on a regular basis. However, if you were noticed because you were different, then that was usually not a good thing as difference was frowned upon and whispered about. As a result, it was expected that you would not do anything that would draw further attention to that difference. In fact, it was expected that you would do everything to minimize the difference and to blend in. A premium was placed upon conformity and acceptance, and the only way to achieve acceptance was to conform.

With that said, I have to admit that there were two things different about me that I was acutely aware of. However, I was fortunate to be able to keep both of these differences from being noticed.

The first difference I will share is that from as far back as I can remember, I have wanted to be in a gun fight. By that I mean I wanted to be in a gun fight like the ones shown in old western movies. The fight where the good guy is really no morally better than the bad guy, but the good guy is perceived as good and he never loses a gun fight. Doc Holliday is a good example and he was my hero, and since I was never in a gun fight, it was easy to keep this different aspect of myself a secret. I did fantasize about it continuously though.

The second difference I will share is that I have always been interested in history and attracted to old things. I know a lot of people have the same interest and the same attraction, and on the surface this does not seem all that different. The fact that many other people could have the same interest and attraction is how I kept this different thing about me from being noticed. However, what made my interest different is the way the old things "spoke" to me. I use that term loosely because no old thing ever said a spoken word to me. Well, my third grade teacher, Mrs. Davis, was an old thing and she spoke to me, but not in the sense that I am talking about here. What I mean is that I could, at times, sense something that I could not explain when I would handle an old artifact, explore an abandoned building or walk across an old battlefield. I could sense the person or people who had used the artifact, or who had lived in the building, or who had fought on the battlefield. The sensation was not frightening. It was more like a lingering residual effect. I once described it to my friend Daisy as being similar to the way I could still smell her perfume on the pillowcase, even if several days had passed since she last slept over. This different aspect was a bit more difficult to keep secret, but I was able to keep it hidden from everyone except her.

1

We had awakened early and had already driven many miles and yet the sun was still in the east. We had travelled in silence, and I felt both a sense of relief and a sense of dread when we reached our destination. I stepped out of the jeep and stared up into another cloudless blue sky. It was then that I realized that I could not remember the last time it had rained. I had been hoping for rain because I thought rain would help soothe the tension, but the rain never came and the tension kept building. The tension between us had now built up to a point that was almost unbearable. It was not the tension of anticipation that builds explosively between two people who know that they are soon to be lovers. It was the tension of resentment that builds over time between two people who no longer understand each other. This tension hung in the air above us like a deep dark cloud, which casts its shadow over all things under it. To make matters worse, I was frustrated with her and she was frustrated with me. I realized, as she stood silently next to me in the bright desert sun, that this frustration was the only thing remaining that we had in common.

We began to unload the jeep together in silence. It was only just after 10:00 in the morning, but it was mid-June and it was dry and it was hot. Which is normal weather this time of year for this area about two hours west of Phoenix, but it seemed particularly hot and dry that day. There was no shade and nothing to produce shade of any substance, just scrub brush and cactus. The rocky side banks of the dry wash a few yards to our right would probably provide some shadowed relief from the sun in the early morning and late afternoon, but at this time of day, even the dry wash was fully exposed and illuminated by the sun's rays. To make matters worse, the sun seemed especially bright and intense as it beat down its rays of focused heat and I could feel my skin burning as if it were melting the shirt on my back. I had not even picked up the shovel and sweat was already running down my face, back, chest and legs. There was no breeze and nothing was moving other than a swarm of black flies, which were buzzing around the blood stained white sheet that covered the body which lay just a few yards behind me. The ground under my boots was baked as hard as concrete.

Daisy was looking at me, expecting an answer to a question that had not been asked. So I gave her the only answer that came to mind. "We bury our dead." I said these four words in a tone of voice that I thought would convey my mood. My mood was that I was not interested in being questioned, or in talking, or in any banter of any type. Evidently, my ability to communicate my mood and feelings still needed a lot more work because she responded right away with a question. I made a mental note to speak to Sam, my counselor, about my continuing inability to communicate and express my feelings.

"Why is that?" She asked in a tone that indicated she did indeed understand the message behind my tone, but was determined to ignore it and let me know that she did not give a damn about my mood.

I turned to face her. She was wearing familiar clothes; clothes that I had seen her wear maybe a hundred times before, but I could not remember a single instance of time or place. Her jeans were tight, dusty, dirty, and threadbare in spots. Her boots reminded me of a photo I once saw of an old Apache woman. Both were brown from exposure to the sun and had that dry wrinkled look that only old boot leather and old facial skin can achieve. Her shirt was cotton flannel and was marked with what was once a checkerboard pattern, but was now just a muddled blend of indistinguishable color. It was buttoned up tight, so that there was no visible cleavage and no chance of any becoming visible. Her light brown hair was pulled back and loosely tied with a yellow piece of cloth. The small scar on her cheek had faded, as had her smile. However, her green-hazel eyes were still bright, piercing, and intelligent.

"We bury our dead out of respect," I finally said.

She pondered that for a few minutes and then asked somewhat sarcastically, "Out of respect for whom? We did not even really know this person. Then we killed him and we sure as hell did not show much respect by doing that. So I don't know why you are so concerned about showing respect now that he is dead and we will never know anything more about him." She was on a roll now and continued, her voice rising. "Plus, I don't really think killing him was something that we had to do. That is now a moot point wouldn't you say?" She raised her eyes to meet mine, and then to briefly scan the horizon, before she returned her gaze to me. She continued, "So here we are, showing our respect by burying this body in an unmarked grave that is miles from nowhere? What kind of respect is that? " She paused again to look over at the bloody sheet before continuing in a softer voice, "Besides, I don't think the dead know that they are dead. Their spirits are gone. All that remains is the body and all it can do is just lie there and rot."

"I don't agree with you about everything that you just said, but now is not the time to discuss our ideas of what the dead know or do not know. However, I will say that we killed him because we had no choice but to kill him. Now go grab that other shovel out of the back of the Jeep and help me dig this hole. I swear with all of these questions, you remind me of your mother."

Her eye flashed anger and she screamed at me, showing real emotion for the first time in a long time. "No choice! Who the hell do you think you are talking to!? Aren't you the one who is always preaching about how life is all about choices? The ones we choose to make and the ones we choose to ignore and the consequences of doing both?" She paused for a second to gesture toward the body with her left hand, "Now we have killed this person that we barely knew, and here we are burying the body in this isolated spot in the middle of fucking nowhere and you are trying to tell me that we had no choice? What the hell is wrong with you?"

When I did not respond, she turned her back to me and said over her shoulder as she walked away, "Well, you and your non-answers. I swear you remind me of every man I have ever known."

I stopped digging long enough to watch her as she walked away. The way her body swayed with each step, the way her arms moved by her side, the pace and length of her steps, even the tilt of her head on her shoulders was a body language that was all too familiar to me. I knew her well and I could tell that she was pissed. As I watched, I realized that I would have been able to tell that she was pissed even if she had never spoken a word before walking away.

She returned with the shovel a few minutes later, tossed a canteen of water in my direction without looking at me, and started to dig. Neither of us spoke for what seemed to be a very long time. The earth was hard and dry and we both struggled with our digging. To this day, I am really not sure how much time passed while the only sounds, besides the incessant buzzing of flies, were the scraping our shovels made as we tried to fill them with the dry dirty dust and pebbles that pass as ground out in the desert, and the sighs and grunts we made as we realized the futility of trying to fill a shovel. It could have been an hour, or it could have been four. Judging by the scant progress we were making, it probably was no more than 15 minutes. I was thinking about giving up on this digging and just leaving the body above ground to rot and provide food for the desert animals and birds.

But the thought was broken by her.

"What about dreams?" she asked in a flat tone of voice.

"What about them?" I asked in return.

"Who buries them when they die"?

"I am not sure I am following you."

"Well, Hank," she said resuming her sarcastic tone from earlier. "It is a pretty straightforward question that I am asking, and people think you are a pretty smart guy. So I don't see what the problem is or what it is that you do not understand;

but let me see if I can make it simpler for you. We are burying this body because it is dead. Wouldn't you say that dreams die too, just as people do? Some grow old, wither, and die. Some die of neglect; some are aborted right after conception; some are killed, and some grow and prosper but are eventually replaced by new dreams, which is a death of sorts. I think that sometimes there is no one to mourn the death of a dream. Just like there is no one to mourn the death of this person we are burying. So, I was just wondering who buries a dream when it is dead?"

I exhaled and gave her a long side glance. I had no answer for this question, and not knowing how to respond, I decided to ignore it by just going back to the digging. After a few moments, I stopped, leaned on the shovel and stared off into the distance. I was looking at nothing in particular as my thoughts started to wander. I returned to my habit of examining choices and their consequences and wondered which choice or series of choices had brought us to this point. As I thought about this, I slowly began to see the pattern and was able to unravel the tangled thread of events along the path that led us here. I ask you to bear with me as it was a circuitous route, lined with memories, adventure stories, and characters from long ago. As I mentally re-traced our steps along this route, I was able to determine, with a good deal of certainty that it was the moment we made the simple choice at a stop sign to turn left instead of right that had brought us here. The story that follows is how it all happened.

2

It was not that long ago, maybe a week, possibly less, but certainly no more than 7 days ago. It is difficult for me to believe that I cannot remember exactly how long ago. I am in the habit of tracking how long almost everything takes and examining the reasons why and the choices that influenced the event. I do it without thinking about it and it is one of those personality traits that some people find endearingly quirky and that others find obnoxiously controlling. However, now I cannot remember how long this last adventure lasted. She and I each had a full 5 days of vacation that we were taking, using the weekend before and after as bookends. That is why I am certain that no more than 7 days elapsed between the time we got lost and our present circumstance of burying this body.

I do remember that it had been mid-day, somewhere between half past 12:00 noon and 1:00.. Which day it was, I cannot remember. It was just another hot, sunny, cloudless day in a line of similar days that are strung together here in the desert southwest and follow one another, until at some point, you no longer even remember the point when one day ends and another begins. Each day blends with the ones that came before and the ones that come after in a pattern of perfect sameness. At times, it is easy to forget that there are places that that do not have such a reliable and repeatable pattern of perfection. Perfection as far as weather is concerned anyway.

I also remember that she was wearing a faded yellow sun dress and was naked underneath. White strappy open toe sandals and a straw hat completed her outfit. Her lips were glossy red and her finger and toenails were painted robin egg blue. It was late spring and she was spring personified.

We had been looking forward to this time away together. It began as most vacations begin; with a discussion of how much of what we packed was needed versus how much of what we packed was wanted. Once this was decided and the bags were loaded, the vacation then took on a feeling of having officially begun. We started out driving, going nowhere in particular, which is something we liked to do whenever we could. It was our way of getting out and unwinding and looking for things or places that we had not seen before, and reconnecting with the desert and with each other. The latter reason was even more important for this trip because our relationship had been on the rocks for the past several months. I was not sure of the reason behind this latest bump in our relationship because it is not like me to ask questions about our relationship, so I just assumed any bumps were my fault and accepted the consequences while attempting to make amends . I was hoping that several days with her away from work would help us get things back on track. As was our custom when we took these trips, we left our mobile phones at home. Nothing interrupts a vacation, or even just a drive in the countryside, more than the incessant alerts of incoming text messages, or emails, or updates from whatever social media you are addicted to. So, our one unbreakable rule when we took these trips was that no mobile devices of any type were allowed.

We had been driving for about two hours, stopping every now and then to take in the view from a scenic overlook, or to get out of the jeep and explore some interesting rock formations, or to take a detour down an unpaved side road just to see where it would lead us. I did not want to admit it then, but my thoughts were not fully on driving due to scantily clad spring personified sitting next to me in the jeep. I had become a little bit turned around and a little confused about exactly where we were. I was not worried about getting lost as it is 2014 and it is almost impossible to get lost when you are near a paved highway these days. Just the same, I really did not know where we were but I did not want to admit to being lost either.

Eventually the hard top unmarked road we were riding on came to an end at a stop sign at a 'T' intersection and a decision had to be made. She wanted to turn left and I thought we would be better off turning right.

We discussed which way to turn and that discussion unfortunately turned into a short but intense argument. In the past, whenever I was lost or unsure and if at the time I had the option between taking either a left hand turn or taking a right hand turn, I would always turn right. I always thought that if I happened to stay lost for some time that it would be better to continue to always turn right at every intersection where a choice had to be made. At least that way I would always be going in a clockwise direction instead of turning left each time, which would take me in a counter-clockwise direction. I had no real facts on which to support this preference other than an article I once read about the Indian Ghost Dance. That dance took place in the late 1800's and, from what I remembered, the dancers always moved in a clockwise circular motion. Doing a ghost dance was never something I had to do, but even if a partial reason the dance moved clockwise was because the dancers felt that was the direction to move in order to get the most benefit, then that was good enough for me. Plus, it just felt right and it felt comfortable to go clockwise whenever in doubt. Some folks would consider this odd, but to me it just seemed like the natural and logical decision to make.

However, this time I turned left simply because she wanted to and I did not feel like arguing about it any longer. My Jeep, that has been my only means of transportation for the last 23 years, gave no protest at all to this change in my driving habits. It occurred to me how much nicer and easier life would be if people were as unconditionally accepting of unexpected change as my jeep was at accepting this change.

The longer I drove, the more this decision weighed on me. It was not long before I started to think about choices, which is another habit of mine that people view in the same way they view my habit of tracking how long things take. I have always found it fascinating to think that every current circumstance or situation in life is determined by some past choice or decision.

It is staggeringly humbling to realize the life changing consequences that have resulted from what seemed at the time to be a random, inconsequential, trivial, or spur of the moment decision. It is equally humbling to realize the relatively small impact that some of the most heart wrenching and tormenting decisions have had. My thoughts carried me back to some of the choices that had led to me driving around this part of the world with this particular woman on this particular day. For example, if I had not made the choices and decisions that led to me dropping out of one college and taking some time off, then I would never have had to make the decision to re-enter a different college a year later. Suppose I had never gone to that different college, then I would not have made the decision to take an English Literature class that was held every Tuesday and Thursday morning from 9:00-11:00. If I had not made the decision to take that particular class at that particular time, then I would not have been around to make the decision to pick up the books that the girl on crutches walking ahead of me dropped as she was leaving class. If I had not made the decision to pick up those books, then I would never have had the conversation that led to the first date with the girl that was to become my first wife. Just to carry this thought further, if I had not made the choices and decisions that brought that life together and eventually led to a divorce, then I would never have been in the situation of having to decide to leave one State and move to another State. If I had not chosen the particular State that I did choose, then it is possible that I would never have been given the choice to work on the Mississippi River. If I had not worked on the River then I would never have had the experience of reading Mark Twain while riding a steamboat paddle wheeler on the Mississippi River. Nor would I have met another special woman. If I had not read that author on that River, then I may have had nothing interesting to break the ice and open a conversation when I met this special woman. If I had not done those things, then I would not have made the decision to move to the West Coast. If I had not moved to the West Coast, then I would not be in this part of the world with this particular woman on this particular day. So, you could say that at least a part of the reason for my current circumstances is that I made the decision to drop out of one college and enter another college way back years ago. I suppose that this train of thought could be carried back even further, all the way to the choices that led my parents to meet and to eventually get married and then to make love on the particular night on which I was conceived. Then extrapolate this thought all the way back to my parents' parents, and so on. In fact, if I carried this thought back far enough, the sheer random luck that I, or any of us, is here may lead to the conclusion that there are really no choices at all and that everything is foreordained. However, I do not really believe that either.

That is just one example of how a series of minor and major decisions and choices lead to a series of life changing circumstances. We like to think that we are in control of our life and decide our fate, which is possibly true for intended consequences. I think that it is the unintended consequences that can end up biting you in the ass. Part of the reason we think we are in control is because we have choices. It is true that in some cases we are fortunate to have a selection of choices to choose from in order to achieve the intended result of shaping the present and the future. Actually, I think that it is the reverse. I have come to think that it is really the choices we make now that decide the future choices that come our way. Here is where the unintended consequences come into the picture. In other words, one initial choice will lead to a whole series of possible choices. If that initial choice had been made differently, then it would be followed by a series of completely different possible choices so that the end resulting circumstance would be entirely different from the current resulting circumstance. Basically, our belief that we are in control because we can choose and decide is like a curtain that hides what lies behind it until it is opened. I think that once that curtain is opened, and what is behind is revealed, it is too late to go back and re-choose. I suspect everyone's life is deceptive like that. As I thought about all of that, the more the decision to turn left back at that 'T' intersection bothered me.

Looking back now, I can see that the left turn we took at that stop sign was the exact decision, and the exact moment, that triggered the chain of events that culminated with us digging a grave in an isolated spot in the desert.

My thoughts were interrupted by her. "My, you are certainly being quiet," she said with a concerned tone. "We are supposed to be out enjoying the day but I can tell that you are distracted."

"Sorry," I said. "I was thinking about choices and the impact they have on our lives."

"Oh no. Please don't start doing that again," she sighed as she rolled her eyes. Then, to irk me, she said the one thing that she knew would irritate me the most. "I try not to make any decisions. Whatever happens, happens," and she said it in a tone that clearly indicated that she had had this conversation with me before and she did not want this conversation to go one word further today.

I picked up on her tone and understood her underlying meaning. So just to piss her off, I continued. "Yes, I know how you feel about making decisions and I know how you feel about even talking about making decisions, but don't you think that taking that approach and not making any decisions and going with whatever happens, happens is also a choice?" I asked. "And don't you think that your decision not to make any decisions is actually a decision unto itself that will eventually lead to a circumstance?"

She became quiet and I could see her out of the corner of my eye and watched as she just turned her head to look out of the jeep window. After a moment, I saw her head turn in my direction and I could feel her eyes on me. I briefly took my eyes off of the road so that I could turn my head to look at her. She was glaring at me. The light in her eyes was blazing and dancing with fire; or maybe it was more of an intense mixture of anger and hurt. Finally, in a sad and exasperated tone, she stated, "I don't understand why you are always examining choices and then talking about the process in the same way that most normal people discuss the weather or sports or God forbid, relationships!" Then, to drive home her point, she continued with her voice taking on a heavier level of sadness, "Our friends don't understand you anymore and that worries me. I don't think I understand you well enough anymore to defend you, and that also worries me. I usually enjoy being with you but I am not sure that I want to continue being put in the position I just described. It is not fair to me and makes me feel uncomfortable."

When I did not respond, she added, "You can be a real dick." She paused for just a second and then added for effect, "And there are times when I think you would be perfectly happy without me."

I just smiled and winked at her.

We drove along in silence for quite some time. I was no longer thinking about choices or about our last conversation, I was now positive that we were lost, and my thoughts focused on trying to figure out where we were. I eventually broke the silence and admitted that by saying, "I think we are lost. I knew I should have turned right and not have made that left turn back there at the intersection."

With a smirk on her face, she said "That was your choice and your decision to do that."

"Not really," I said. Keeping to myself the thought that I turned left only because she wanted to and if I had been alone then I would have turned right. "But it is obvious now to see that that decision to turn left has put us in this unintended consequence of being lost. Which I believe makes my point." With a frown, I pulled off to the side of the road and stopped the jeep. Using the running board as a booster step, I climbed up on the hood, burning my hands on the metal as I did so. I scanned the horizon looking for something recognizable or some clue to tell me where we may be, but all I saw were patches of shadow and sunlight falling across an unpainted, hard top cracked asphalt road that stretched off endlessly ahead of us and behind us into the desert horizon.

As I stood on the hood looking at our surroundings, I was struck by how this current situation reminded me of some of the post-apocalyptic scenes that I had seen on TV and at the movies. There had not been any apocalypse. As far as I knew, the world was still populated with living beings. There were not any walking dead zombies, or vampires, or any other mutated winged creatures from Hell stalking us. We were simply lost. I took some comfort in knowing that we were well armed and well acquainted with the use of our firearms. I carried a classic style Colt 45 single action revolver in a leather gun belt and holster around my waist. The gun was loaded with 5 rounds, the chamber opposite the firing pin being empty for safety reasons. The gun belt carried an additional 25 rounds in holders sewn into the leather. I knew that she also has a Bond Snake Slayer Derringer in a pocket holster that she usually carried tucked into her clothing or against her body, but knowing that she was just wearing a sun dress and nothing else, I was momentarily distracted thinking about where she could possibly be carrying it today. She kept it loaded with one .45 caliber long colt cartridge and one 410 gauge shotgun shell, 00 buck of course. It only had an accurate range of about 20 feet, but was powerful enough to ruin anyone's day within that range. I was certain that she had a couple of reloads stashed somewhere else on her body. So, between the two of us, we could get off 7 quick shots if need be and then also be able reload if we had to work our way back to the jeep where an assortment of other .45 caliber handguns, a stagecoach shotgun, and 1100 rounds of the appropriate cartridges and shells were stored in the back under a layer of blankets and bags. So, any Dead Walkers had better think twice about coming after us. There was even a Henry model .45 caliber lever action rifle for long distance shooting. I once heard some old cowboy in a Western movie say that he did not expect trouble, but if trouble happened, then he did not want to get killed for a lack of being able to shoot back. I suppose that philosophy has stuck with me.

I stood there for a few moments longer looking out across the desert landscape and reflecting on it. A lot of people look at this landscape and think it ugly and barren, but I find it beautiful in a direct, no nonsense sort of way. The rocky hills add contour and shape to the flatness. The brilliant cloudless powder blue sky above adds contrast to the black, tan, brown, and muted green colors that are the desert floor. The plants and cactus that grow seem to defy the harshness of their environment and thrive on it. I have seen cactus grow at crazy angles in nothing more than a crack between two rocks, where the rocks are too hot to touch and the crack appears to offer nothing for the cactus to anchor itself to. It is almost as if the rock supports the cactus by itself and it is understood that is the way it will be. It is as if the cactus understands that if it wants to live and grow here then it will accept only what the rock can offer and expect nothing more. There are animals and birds and reptiles that live here too, all of them living and surviving only on what little is offered. The desert does not pretend to be something it is not. It offers itself to you and invites you in but only on its terms. It is beautiful and deadly, and it calls to some of us. Those of us who answer its call understand the terms and accept them. The rewards are many, but you have to be smart and you have to be prepared. Everything in the desert can hurt you, or even kill you, if you are clumsy, or disrespectful, or if you simply do not pay attention.

I have made a few excursions into the desert without her. I thought of my friend Sandy as I stood on the hood of my jeep and I was reminded of one of these other trips. Sandy had a UTV and we would tow it behind the jeep until we found a suitable place to unhitch it. Then we would use it to ride old stagecoach or horse trails, explore old mines, look for artifacts, prospect, or just to get out for a day in search of a little adventure. Usually, these went without incident as we were careful and respected the elements. We would sometimes get lost for a period of time but always found our way back. It was, however, a very noisy vehicle and that made conversation difficult.

One trip we made was memorable for the sights we saw and also for the danger that was present. We came upon this small shady glade that was sheltered by high cliffs. It was a surprising find. The air was many degrees cooler than the open desert we had just ridden through, and there were cottonwood trees and flowering plants growing in the soil. There was even a small well that had been built by some long gone old time inhabitant. However, the sight that stopped us was the thousands of butterflies fluttering under the cottonwood trees and across the open areas in an unbelievable sight of beauty and freedom. I am not sure what kind of butterflies these were, but the air was alive with the movement of their yellow, orange, and black wings. There were also many wasps and these were huge, about the size of dragonflies. They were drawn to the water and we were fortunate that they were not interested in us. I have noticed before that regardless of where you may be in the desert, if you open a water bottle and leave it open, that it does not take long for wasps and bees to come around. They are able to sense water and they appear to come out of nowhere to investigate. Mixed in with these butterflies and wasps were several Tarantula Hawks. These would glide past in their peculiar way of flying, looking like some pre-historic bug that had time travelled to the present in order to investigate its modern day insect cousins. If you have never seen a Tarantula Hawk, then you should look one up. I believe they are truly the most frightening looking insect I have ever seen. I have heard that when these Hawks sting someone, the pain is so intense that all the person can do is screaming.

Sandy stopped the UTV but kept the engine running. We sat for a few minutes looking at this unexpected beauty. At some point, I happened to look down. The UTV was open air and the floor of the vehicle only cleared the ground by about 12 inches. I was just wearing tennis shoes and shorts. When I looked down, there was a rattlesnake whose head was no more than 10 inches away from my right foot. We had not heard its warning rattle because the UTV was so loud. The snake was curled into a striking position with its rattle erect and shaking behind its head. I do not know where it was looking before I noticed it, but now its eyes were looking directly into mine as its tongue flicked the air. I suppose the UTV must have confused it because there is no other explanation for why it had not already bitten me. I was afraid to move and I was afraid not to move. I was completely frozen. Eventually, I tried to get Sandy's attention but he was preoccupied with looking at the butterflies and the engine was so loud that he could not hear me unless I shouted, which I did not want to do. I knew it was only a matter of time before he started the UTV moving again, or stopped the engine altogether and started moving himself, and I was afraid that either of these actions would make the snake strike out at me. So, I slowly moved my hand down to my single action Colt 45 that I had strapped in a holster on my right leg. I pulled the hammer back to full cock as I ever so slowly slid the gun upwards until the barrel had cleared the holster. Then without raising the gun any more than necessary, I pointed it down my leg towards what I hoped was the snake's head and not my foot. When I thought I had the correct aim, I pulled the trigger and the bullet hit the snake in the body about 3 inches below his mouth. Not completely on target but it got the job done. The gun shot scared the crap out of Sandy. He was startled so badly that he jumped a couple of feet and almost fell out of the UTV. I got a pretty good laugh out of that. From the time I saw the snake until the time I shot it, probably less than thirty seconds passed, but it seemed like a lifetime. That is an excellent lesson of what can happen when you become distracted and let your guard down in the desert. We were fortunate to get away without injury.

Sandy and I had other interesting adventures as well. Like the time we were looking at an old map which showed an area where a town once existed. Upon further research, we learned that the entire town burned down in the 1880's and was never rebuilt. The survivors had simply picked up, moved somewhere else, and started over. That sounded like something fun to explore, so we got the coordinates and went looking for it in the UTV. To our dismay, there was absolutely nothing left of it. If we had not had the map and the coordinates we would never have known that a town used to stand on the spot. The land was gently rolling, and the slopes of the hill and the ground at the base of the hill were bare of any indication of human habitation. The only thing we did find was a small cemetery. It was badly neglected of course. The rusted and twisted remains of an ornate wrought iron fence that had once enclosed the graveyard could still be seen in spots. The graveyard itself was wildly overgrown with weeds, and thorn-bushes, and cactus and was almost impossible to walk through. I thought that the thorn-bushes could have been the descendants of rose bushes that had been thoughtfully planted as memorial decorations generations ago, but now they were just unkempt thorn-bushes gone wild. In addition, the ground had been washed out where water had run down the hill and carved gullies through the graveyard. Here and there, coffin nails could be seen lying on the ground but no bones were visible. Only two headstones had markings whose words could still be read. These two headstones were made of polished black marble and carved with the names of a man and his wife. They had died about a year apart and about a decade before the fire that destroyed the town. From the fact that they had marble markers, it seemed likely that they had been from one of the town's more well-to-do families or at least they had been respected by the town's people. The majority of the grave markers would have been handmade crosses of wood and had rotted away long ago. Other than those two, the few other stone grave markers that survived were made of limestone and were illegible. Some of these were still standing, but most were broken and just lying on the ground or askew in the gullies. On one of the black marble markers, the words "Loving husband, Father, and Friend, Gone but not forgotten" had been carved under the man's name followed by his date of birth and death. It struck me as I read those words just how fleeting life is, because I was pretty sure he had been forgotten. He had been forgotten long ago; so had his wife, and so had the remains of every other body that lay under the ground in that graveyard. I remember that the graveyard itself even felt dead and forgotten. It was as if even the spirits of these forgotten folks had also died or had at least moved on somewhere else when the town moved on. I was pretty sure that everyone buried here was gone and forgotten. It was a sad place.

But there are other stories I could tell. Such as the time we found these amazing Anasazi Indian ruins with petro glyphs on the walls and artifacts lying on the ground. These ruins were on National Park land but were unmonitored, except for a posted sign that announced these were park lands and to not touch anything. Or the time we explored a dry river bed for miles and miles and found the dry mummified remains of animals, along with other items. Or maybe you'd like to hear about the time we attempted to cross a flooded wash that almost drowned us both. Or maybe the time we came across an old army cavalry outpost, whose walls were built with stones that had been carried by hand to a spot on a hill overlooking a small river valley and there assembled into the outpost. That outpost dates back to the 1870's, when General George Crook was hunting and fighting small bands of Indians in the Arizona Territory, which was about the same time that General George A. Custer was hunting and fighting larger bands of Indians on the plains further north in the Montana and Dakota Territories. Those are all good stories, but I will not go into them in detail at this time. These other stories will have to wait for another opportunity. I only mention them now so that you will know that this adventure was not my first into the desert. It was, however, the most unusual and the most enlightening.

3

I realized that I had been standing on the hood for several minutes longer than I should have and I also knew that I needed to come down and explain our situation to her. I climbed down from the hood, being careful this time not to burn my hands, and walked around behind the Jeep. The front windshield was made of glass and the top of the jeep was canvas. The rest of what served as windows on the jeep was just clear plastic attached to the frame and roll bar. When I reached the back of the jeep, I unzipped a portion of the plastic that served as the rear window, reached in, and grabbed a canteen of water out of the back. Then, coming back around to the passenger side, I looked in at her sitting in the passenger seat. When she did not return my look, I continued walking off the road and into the brush and kept walking until I was almost out of sight. I stopped when I reached a 40 foot tall multi-arm Saguaro cactus. As I studied the trunk of this giant, my thoughts were drawn to the sights that this old cactus had seen. It had been standing here from the days before Arizona was a state. Maybe it had been standing here from as far back as when wild Indians were the only humans passing through; before the Spanish explorers on horseback came seeking gold and silver; before lonely white riders would pass by on their quest to seek a path further west; before the troops of cavalry chased away any remaining Indians in an attempt to make this part of the country safe for settlers; before stagecoach passengers came with the intent of prospering from what the ones who came before them had built; up to the motorized people of today who are too comfortable in their transit to take the time to stop and look. I unzipped my jeans to take a leak. As the urine began to puddle and sink into the dry caked dirt, I noticed that about a half of a dozen bees had appeared and were crawling around the edge of the puddle of piss. I was once again amazed at how these insects can sense and find any type of water and then appear out of nowhere to investigate. While watching the bees, I glimpsed movement out of the corner of my eye off to the right. I turned my head to look and saw two Hummingbirds flitting around the bright yellow blossoms of a Lantana bush. Off to the side of the bush, I noticed what appeared to be a worn path winding up the slight hill. Following the path with my eyes, I noticed some old rusted cans lying around. I recognized their size and shape from similar cans I had seen on the desert floor on previous adventures and I knew that these cans were fairly old and were made to contain lard compound. They were a little smaller than a modern day gallon bucket of paint, and even though they were rusted and pitted, the name that was stamped into them could usually still be read. It was usually "Ivory Brand" lard a compound made by The Cudahy Packaging Co. from Omaha or lard compound from the Armour Packaging Co. from Kansas City. These were two big suppliers from back in the 1890's, and throughout the early 1900's, and their rusted metal cans still lie on the desert floor and still carry their imprinted name over 120 years later. I noticed other, now useless, manmade artifacts that had also been discarded long ago and which were lying amongst the lard cans and strewn alongside the path. I knew from experience that these artifacts meant that there was probably an old abandoned mine and maybe even the remains of miner's shack nearby. I knew she would be excited about the possibility of exploring this and I made a mental note to mention it to her when I returned to the jeep.

My eyes followed the worn path all the way to the top of the hill where the crest met the brilliant blue of the desert sky. Just over the crest I could see a lone hawk circling and hunting, using its laser sharp vision to detect a victim. I gave my penis a few quick shakes and pulls to squeeze out any remaining urine and as I did so my eyes focused back on the hummingbirds in the Lantana bush. I called out over my shoulder to her, "Hey, do you remember the river back in Virginia?" I had taken her to Virginia a few years prior. She had wanted to see the town I had grown up in and she had wanted to explore the Civil War battlefields in the surrounding area. I do not remember if she responded to my question. If she did, I did not hear her answer as my thoughts had already carried me back there.

The Nottoway River literally ran through the backyard of the house I grew up in. This had some obvious, and not so obvious, pros and cons. One drawback was that our backyard was under water every time the river overflowed its banks, which happened several times each year. Another drawback was that there were always snakes in the yard and around the house, particularly water moccasins. We all were taught at an early age to always look before you stepped when in the backyard. We were also taught at an early age how to use a gun and encouraged to always either carry one or have one nearby. Having the river in the backyard provided opportunities for adventure and imagination, and as a result, I spent many hours exploring its banks and sandbars. The best time for exploring was during the summer, when the water level would usually drop dramatically and I was able to wade to areas that would be covered by water several feet over my head during the rest of the year. It was on this river that my father would take me fishing. We would usually go in the early morning before his work day and my school day started, or we would go in the late afternoon after each had ended. On rare occasions we would go in the middle of the day. The elementary school I attended was right across the street from our house. Every day at lunch time I would walk across the street from the school yard to home and eat the sandwich that my mother had made for me. On the days when we would go fishing in the middle of the day, I would not return to school after lunch. As much of a treat as that was to skip an afternoon of school, early morning was my favorite time to go fishing. We would get up before dawn and untie the boat from the tree that held it secure against the river current. We would use the paddle to push out away from the river bank and then start the in-board/outboard motor and head upriver away from town. As we got further from town, the river banks would gradually become less steep and the distance between the weather-beaten houses of the people would increase. Back in town, the distance between houses was a few hundred feet or so, but as we passed the town limits, the distance would increase by many hundreds of feet. Then, once away from town completely, the distance between houses would be measured in miles. The houses up on the banks would still be dark and presented a peaceful image as the inhabitants would still be sleeping. As if not to disturb the scene, even the dogs in the yard would not bark as we went past. They would only lift their heads and sniff the air, satisfied that we presented no threat and were just passing through their domain.

One thing these little fishing trips instilled in me at a very young age is that the past is all around us. It lies partially hidden in plain sight, just beneath the surface of our everyday existence. All you have to do is take the time to listen and look and you will find it. Or maybe more appropriately, it will find you.

The main channel of the river had many small branches that would run inland for some distance. These always seemed like ideal places to explore and sometimes, when the fish were not biting, we would enter one of these branches and follow it until the end. Occasionally, we would drift past the remains of old farm homes that dated back to before the Civil War. As we would glide along, sometimes my dad would stop the boat and we would get out and explore. All of these old homes were in ruins and some had been vacant for decades. The original owners had left after the war, either because all of the men had been killed, or because the family had lost everything, or a combination of both. These were not grand plantations; they were just your average farm where the inhabitants survived and prospered to the extent necessary to maintain that survival. They were certainly not wealthy. According to my father, most of these families worked the land themselves and owned few, if any, slaves. He also said that there were families like this throughout the area and throughout the entire South; but still the men chose to fight for the Confederate States, and their families and their descendants suffered the consequences of that choice.

The silent walls and chimneys that sometimes still stood, and the broken down doors and vacant windows that sometimes still remained of these buildings were sad reminders of that time. I can remember looking at these ruins and walking among them. Even now, I can recall how sad they made me feel and I remember I could sense the people who had once lived here. I felt their presence as I walked amongst the ruins and I could sense their struggle as their lives were being destroyed. I knew the people had left in a time of great sadness and sorrow amidst death and destruction. To me, it felt as if all of that sadness and sorrow had been too great for the buildings that were left behind to bear, so the bitterness had overflowed the confines of the buildings and seeped into the very ground, where it cried out through the silence seeking solace and defying anyone to forget what had happened there. The tormented spirit of these ruins was deep and palpable. It was almost as if the ruins were weeping. As we walked among them, I would look for something to connect me further to the people from that time, but I seldom found anything. Although on one of these side trips, I did find a small lockbox that was filled with paper Confederate money under the floorboards of one of these houses. Many years have passed since these days, but I still remember that when I saw the box, I also sensed the woman who had placed the box there. She was middle aged, white, and maybe once attractive. Her home spun cotton skirt was too long for her and the frayed hem dragged the floor. The plain sweater she wore was too small for her and the sleeves did not quite reach her wrists. Her face was round and pleasant and she had soft blue eyes. Her light brown hair was cut so short that if I had only seen her head I may have thought that I was looking at a boy. Her lips were pressed so tightly together that they creased, and her mouth was turned down into what appeared to be a permanent frown. Her hands were dirty and the skin on them was so thin that it was almost transparent. They shook slightly and she attempted to smile as she lowered the box and replaced the floor boards. I sensed that she was fragile and that she was sick and that she lived alone and it had been years since she had seen her husband who had gone off to fight.. The box contained about fifteen bills of $1 and $2 denominations. They were in fairly good condition given they had been buried for over one hundred years, but they proved to be worthless. I still have them.

Other times, we would tie the boat to a tree and get out and walk the corn or peanut or soybean fields that bordered the river in places. We would find arrowheads and pottery shards left by the native Indians that lived along the river banks hundreds of years earlier. These Indians were the Cheroenhaka tribe, which eventually became known as the Nadawa and were then called Nottoway by the colonials. These Indians lodged and hunted in the southeastern part of Virginia and were eventually pushed out by the arriving colonials. Sometimes, when it was very quiet on the river, I thought I could hear the old Indians moving around in the woods, hidden by the mists. Out of the corner of my eye, I would sometimes catch an impression of movement, but when I would turn to look the image would melt away. I never saw any Indian ghosts and for some reason, I was never able to connect the way I could with others who had passed, but I was sure that they were there, watching us.

When we reached what my dad had determined was to be that day's fishing spot, he would stop the motor and let the current drift the boat as we fished for Red Throat. The river was quiet and still and partly covered by a wispy foggy mist that would sometimes reach up high into the trees. The only sounds were the noise of the water as it glided past our boat and the calls of the birds and animals from deep in the forest. In some places, the river banks were low and the forest came right down to the water's edge. During the rainy season, the water would be many feet higher and everything I was looking at then would be underwater, but on those days, I could look deep into the forest where land and river mixed into swamp. The water was the color of strong iced tea. The air would be warm, thick, heavy, and would become stifling as morning turned into afternoon. There was the pungent smell of damp river mud, insects, and rotting vegetation. I could see the cypress tree roots sticking out of the water and looking like the elbows and knees of some disjointed submerged giant. It felt to me like I was looking at a landscape that had not changed since creation. It was on one of these mornings that I noticed two Bluebirds on a branch of a tree overhanging the river. I always sat in the front of the boat and my dad would sit in the back where the motor and boat paddle were, in case we needed either. I watched the birds for a few moments and then, without turning around to look at my dad, I asked him if he ever thought about bird pussy. Without hesitation, he said, "Only when I cannot think of anything else to think of." Then, a moment later he followed with, "Why do you ask a question like that"?

"Because I have been thinking about girls a lot lately," I said. To add further clarification just in case he did not get my point, I added "And the girls are naked."

"I see," he said.

When I did not respond, he continued, "Is that all?"

I could feel my face getting red, but I had started this conversation and I knew he would make me continue it until I had completed my thought. "No, sir." I said. "Not quite. You see, I was watching these two birds up on that limb over there and I was just wondering if boy birds have the same thoughts about girl birds and if they think about how to get some bird pussy."

After a moment he said, "There is no way to know for sure what they think about. There is really no way to know for sure if they even think in a way that you and I would consider thinking. I suppose they have desires or instincts or drives that lead the boy birds to seek out girl birds. I suppose it is possible that no thoughts occur at all and it is something that is just naturally done. In any event, I doubt the boy bird ever thinks about bird pussy in the same way that you think about girl pussy. Does that help explain it?" he asked.

"Not really," I said.

"Well, that is ok. I was a young boy once and I also spent a lot of time thinking about things of little importance and no merit. You'll understand what I mean one day and then you will begin to see things in a different way," he said.

He had no idea how right he was.

4

Once again my thoughts were interrupted by her. The sharp sound of the jeep's horn followed by her voice took me away from my thoughts and brought me back to the present.

"Are you going to stand there and piss all day, or are you just playing with that thing now"? She yelled with obvious irritation.

"I am almost done but my arms are getting tired. Do you want to come hold it for me?" was my response.

She did not respond of course, so I gulped down the rest of the water in the canteen, tucked myself back into my jeans, and zipped up. Then, with one last look back at the Hummingbirds, I turned and headed towards her and the Jeep.

As I got closer to the jeep, I could hear the irritation still in her voice when she asked, "Just what were you doing over there that took so long?"

I walked up and leaned my head through her open window. She was still on the passenger side, but was now sitting in the seat with her legs crossed Indian style. The hem of her sun dress was about three quarters of the way up her thighs and it was wonderfully obvious that she was wearing nothing under it. She noticed that my eyes were not on her eyes and she uncrossed her legs and tugged her dress down.

I moved my gaze up to her eyes and said, "Nothing much, playing with myself, taking a piss and reliving a memory."

"That's nice, just another day in paradise. I was beginning to think that maybe we were just going to sit here by the road for the rest of the day and watch the shadows grow, but I am glad you were productive and enjoyed yourself," was her rapid and sarcastic response. She paused, broke eye contact with me, and then asked, "What kind of memory?"

"Ah, nothing you'd be interested in," I said. I regretted my answer immediately because I knew that she would interpret my quick answer as a brush off, and that would result either in her becoming defensive or in her becoming more irritated.

"Don't be so sure," she said firmly. "Sometimes I find your old stories and memories entertaining."

"Old, huh? Well, maybe so, but I don't think you would like this one."

"Why not?" she quickly responded, her eyes flashing. "I am able to decide for myself what I like and what I don't like, so let me hear it."

"No. It is more of a guy memory," I said, becoming defensive now myself. "And you would neither like it nor understand it."

"Oh, I see." She said, now clearly beyond being just merely irritated. "All that means is that the memory is either gross, disgusting, stupid, demeaning or all of those things at once. I swear, men are so transparent and dumb. When I was younger, my girlfriends and I were so curious and intrigued about what guys do and think about. We would actually spend time trying to think of ways to get a guy's attention so that we could talk and figure him out. That was time wasted, and it did not take us long to discover the answer to what you guys think about. By the time our first dates were half over, we knew. From that point forward, we understood that there is only one thing that men want. We also realized that we had it; and more importantly, that were in control of it. Then, it was game over and we knew we had men screwed, both literally and figuratively. Most people put a lot of value on gold and diamonds and things like that; but there is nothing more valuable than the treasure us girls have between our legs. You, Doc, unknowingly just proved my point a few minutes ago when you stuck your fat head inside the window and your eyes focused on my pussy before you looked at my eyes or even spoke a word. Pussy is pretty much the only thing that every non-gay guy on the planet will do whatever we want in order to get. You know it, I know it, everyone knows it; but no one talks about it or acknowledges it. Men have stolen, fought, killed, lied, cheated, begged, married, divorced, re-married, and paid for it. It has always been this way and will always be this way. I will also say that there is nothing that anyone can do about it."

She finished and I was silent for several moments. During that silence, I realized that, other than the part about my head being fat, most of what she had said was absolutely correct. I finally broke the silence by saying, "That was well said and very insightful. I see you learned well. I guess you think you have it all figured out now, huh?"

"Yes. I had a very good role model to teach me," was her answer. She paused briefly to brush her hair out of her eyes and then continued, "But I am learning that there may be some men and some things that cannot really ever be fully understood or controlled or explained. Like everything else in life, there are exceptions that do not fit into any preconceived box and these exceptions cannot ever be anything but an exception. For some reason, it is those exceptions that I find most interesting and appealing."

I smiled at her for the first time since returning to the jeep, and said, "For some reason, it does not surprise me to hear you say that." Also for the first time, she returned my smile.

We remained in silence for a few minutes. I don't think either of us knew exactly what to say next. I was kicking some dirt around with the toe of my boot and thinking about the path and the artifacts I had seen. As usual when we were not talking about relationships or being sarcastic, I spoke first. "While I was over there taking a piss, I noticed a path and some cast away metal leading up that hill. I think there may be an old mine and possibly the remains of an old mining camp nearby. Since we really have nowhere special to go and since we are lost anyway, how about we take a little time and explore what might be over that hill?"

Her eyes lit up. She may be a pain in the ass most of the time, but a chance to have a little adventure and explore some old ruins would always get her attention. It was guaranteed that she would be interested and it was the one thing that endeared her most to me. Before I could react, she moved to open her door just as I was in the process of stepping away. However, she was quicker in opening than I was in stepping and the edge of the door caught me just under my left knee cap and I dropped like a rock.

"Fucking hell," I gasped as I clutched my knee.

She was so excited that she did not notice what had happened. "Are you ok, what is wrong?" she asked over her shoulder as she walked toward the back of the jeep.

"You slammed the door into my knee," I said.

"Oh geez, is that all"? she asked. The lack of compassion in her voice was overwhelming. "I thought you had a heart attack or something the way you were carrying on. Can you stand?"

I held onto the side of the jeep for balance and pulled myself up. I stood there for a moment rubbing the knee and moving the cap from side to side gently. "Yes, I can stand," I finally said.

Satisfied with my answer, she continued on towards the back of the jeep, stepping out of her sun dress as she turned the corner out of sight. She unzipped the back window and pulled out the canvas bag that she always carried and which contained a change of clothes for her. She quickly pulled on her jeans and an old checkered flannel shirt. She pulled her hair back and replaced the straw hat with a baseball cap. Then she came back around to where I was standing and sat down on the ground and put on her socks and her boots. Only when the boots were tightly laced up and tied did she look up at me and speak. "Good. I don't see any blood and it does not look to be dislocated. Just rub some dirt on it and you'll be fine. Let's go."

And with that, we headed back into the brush and towards the path I had seen.

We followed it for about 200 yards, up the hill and back down. There were the usual signs of past human activity including the standard rusted cans that I have already mentioned, rusted bed springs, rusted nails, old rotten wooden boards, discarded shell casings, etc. There was basically nothing of value and a nightmare for a man with a metal detector. At the bottom of the first small rise, the path turned and followed the base of the next hill where we came upon the remains of what was once a three room shack. What the rooms once were is anyone's guess, possibly nothing more than a bedroom, a room for cooking, and a store room. The walls were made of stacked rock and were mostly intact. The roof had caved in long ago, and there were only empty holes in the walls to mark where the door and two windows had once been. Now these holes only served as a portal from the empty vastness of the outside to the empty desolation of the inside. It is possible that the windows were once enclosed, but I did not see the remains of any glass. So, they could have been open windows with only wooden shutters or they could have been covered with just a piece of cloth. We entered through the hole that had once been the door and poked around the base of the walls and eves hoping to find something, but as usual there was nothing.

There are the remains of shacks like this one all over the desert. I have seen remains similar to this one several times before. They are always pretty much the same; solitary buildings that used to hold solitary lives. All that remains now is the ruins of the buildings, but there is no record of what happened to the lives that once shared this isolated existence. One thing for sure is that the people who once inhabited these shacks lived in constant and continuous contact with the elements and became one with them. The harshness and the struggle were as much a part of their daily lives as the internet and electricity are a part of our daily lives today. Imagining what their daily lives were like is difficult but it can be imagined with a little effort. Actually, understanding what their lives were like is almost beyond imagination. It is difficult to fully and realistically understand a life where everything was a chore that had to be planned and done in order to survive, and usually had to be done with no help. Even obtaining a basic necessity, such as water, required planning and effort. The water had to be found, a vessel to hold and carry it then had to be made or obtained, and then a place to store it and protect had to be built. I realized that such basic chores as this had to be done every single day without fail and that was just securing water. Once that was done, there was food that had to be hunted or grown; then prepared and cooked and preserved. Then, there was always the task of being on the lookout for predators, both human and animal. If these things were not enough of a full time job, then there was the added task of prospecting for gold or silver, which is why these people came here and chose this life in the first place. Nothing came easy to these people. Even death did not come easy. Death was common, but it was not easy. It was violent or painful or both, but it was never easy.

She walked back outside to look around and left me standing in the ruins of the shack. I tried to imagine what the three rooms could have been used for and, as I did, the person who once struggled here appeared. I saw him standing in the hole in the wall where the door once was. Unlike most of the visions I see, this one actually looked at me. Not only did his gaze meet mine but he looked at me with an expression that said, "You wanted to see me, so here I am. Take a good look son and then leave me alone." His mouth gaped open and the few teeth he had were stained gray and yellow and looked to have never been touched by a brush. He was filthy and it was obvious that his neglect to wash his body was second only to his neglect to brush his teeth. I was relieved that my vision did not involve my sense of smell. He was skinny, and he looked malnourished and bone tired. He also looked unsociable and uncomfortable. His clothes were just a step above rags and were barely enough to hide his nakedness. His body was bent and twisted from overwork and it carried the scars and scabs of numerous mishaps and insect bites. His hands were rough and cracked; his fingernails were black and broken. What looked like a tin spoon, with a short piece of rope tied around the handle, dangled from his left hand. He did not take a step, but I got the impression that he would have walked with a slight limp. His hair and whiskers were a dark mass of tangles that covered a face that was long and unattractive. His brown eyes were deep, sun burned, and untrusting. He seldom spoke to another human, but I got the sense that he talked out loud regularly to himself and to the rocks and hills and stars. I thought that at some point he once had a half wild coyote as a companion, but changed my mind as a companion did not seem important to him. If I were to actually meet him, I would think that he was crazy. He probably was, but in a canny way. His mind was keen and quick, and he knew what he needed to know and he knew what he needed to do in order to survive. It is quite probable that he thought more like a criminal than a laborer. If he believed in God, then it was so he would have someone to blame when things went bad. When things went well, he knew it was only because of his own hard work, and he gave all the credit to himself. The shack, which was his only refuge, had been vermin and rodent ridden as well. That was the impression he conveyed to me, and then he was gone.

It occurred to me that life back then was so different from life today, that if you were to able to transport back in time to those days, then it is possible you would think you had landed on another planet. Of course, if we wanted to actually experience something similar to that sort of life then we could sign up and pay a fortune for one of those adventure vacations that deprive you of every comfort and convenience that you have worked your whole life to achieve, so that you can live like people did before such comforts and conveniences were available. That really does not make much sense to me. Especially when at the end of it you can escape and return to modern day life and the conveniences and comforts that we have come to take for granted. The man who once lived here, and all of those like him, had no comfort and no conveniences; their only escape was to strike it rich or die.

The sound of her footsteps crunching on the dry dirt outside the walls of the shack brought me back to the present. I took one last look around the abandoned interior and then bid the old man a silent goodbye as I gingerly stepped through the doorway, where he had been standing when he appeared to me, and headed back out into the world.

She was carefully poking around in a pile of refuge that probably held nothing but black widow spiders and scorpions; you never know what may lie hidden underneath the surface of anything unless you poke around a little.

"Find anything?" I calmly asked.

"Nothing valuable, just the usual junk," she said. Then she added, "I did find this piece of wood lying about 20 yards from the shack down in that small wash." She waved her arm and pointed toward some vague spot behind the shack. "It was just lying on the ground and appeared to have a name and a date or at least some letters and some numbers carved into it, but it was pretty badly worm eaten and just disintegrated into pieces when I tried to pick it up to get a closer look. All I could make out were what looked like the letter C, and then a letter that I could not make out which was followed by the letter R, and then several other letters that I could not read. Then, what looked like four numbers were under the letters. I think I could make out the number 8, but that is just a guess as it fell apart when I tried to get a closer look. It is amazing that it had lasted this long out here and it would have been interesting to know what the letters and numbers were, but it is gone now." "How about you?" she asked without looking at me.

"Ah no, nothing, there was nothing interesting in the shack. Not a damn thing at all interesting in there." I said.

She gave me a quizzical look. I knew she suspected that I had seen something in the shack, but she did not question me. All she said was, "Ok. What do you want to do now?" It was more of a statement than a question.

"Well." I lifted my head and moved my eyes around, scanning the area and looking at everything except her, avoiding her eyes. I had my back to her when I continued, "There is really nothing more to see here. The opening to the old mine shaft is probably nearby. It could be around the base of this hill or the next one. Since we are here, we could follow the base of this hill around and check it out if you want. Or we could head back to the jeep and see if we can figure out where we are. It does not matter to me either way, the choice is yours to make."

I turned to look at her for her answer, but she was already moving toward where the path turned and disappeared as it rounded the base of the hill. I suppose it was her way of trying to make her point that she does not make choices but goes with her whatever happens, happens way of thinking.

I gave another look back at the ruined shack, halfway expecting to see the old miner watching me from the doorway, but all I saw of that hard life were the crumbled walls that once had sheltered it.

Turning back, I saw her just as she disappeared around the base of the hill, "Hey!! Wait up," I called out to her and trotted after her.

I caught up to her just as she was rounding the turn at the bottom of the hill. We walked side by side as we followed the path that now headed slightly downward. The sides of the hill were becoming more jagged rock and cliff-like, instead of the smooth round rocky slopes on the previous hill. The geology was just a little bit different here than it was back where we left the jeep. The land was still dotted with saguaro and ocotillo but the rocks were noticeably different. Some of the rocks had a greenish tint from oxidized copper and as we rounded the next bend we saw a long vein of quartz running along the upper edges of the hill side. We knew we had to be getting close to the old mine.

The path leveled out and then began to rise slightly. As we got near the top of the next small rise, the atmospheric pressure abruptly changed. We actually felt the sound vibrate deep in our chests and press against our temples before we heard it with our ears. It was as if a giant mechanical wheel was running somewhere ahead of us, making the air hum and vibrate as it spun. It was only when we reached the top of the rise that it became clear what we had found. The vibration we felt, and could now hear quite well, was caused by thousands if not tens of thousands of bees. We could see them flying in and out and around a hole in the hill about 30 or 40 yards ahead of us. The hole was the entrance to the old mine and probably led down an unknown depth, but somewhere in that depth these bees had built a hive, and by the sound it must have been a monstrous one. It was either monstrous, or it could have just sounded that way because the rock walls of the mine shaft amplified the sound and the vibration being produced. I had no intention of getting any closer to find out which it was.

We had only been standing at the crest observing this sight for a few seconds before the bees noticed us and some came our way and started buzzing around us in warning. You hear stories from time to time about people and their pets being attacked by a swarm of bees. It is not all that common, but it does happen, especially in the spring and summer. Sometimes, the result is fatal to the person or animal. I am not sure if anyone knows exactly what causes a swarm to attack. The most obvious reason is the person or animal unintentionally stumbled upon a hive and then did something to alarm the bees. No one really knows for sure because sometimes the victim of the attack says that he was simply walking along the sidewalk and the bees came out of nowhere and attacked with no provocation. The mistake made is that once the bees start swarming, the person would make the situation worse by going into a panic and would attempt to try to fight off the bees, which in turn makes the bees feel more threatened and become more aggressive, which in turn would make the person fight harder in an epic struggle for survival or escape. Just to add more horror to a bee attack, a swarm cannot be outrun or outfought. And if you try to escape by jumping into a pool or pond and going under water, the bees know you are there and will wait for you to surface.

Regardless of why these attacks happen, I knew right away that we were in serious trouble. She was headstrong and brave and never one to back down from a fight, but she did have one crippling weakness and that was her abnormal fear of bees. The moment we crested that small rise and saw what was causing the vibration, she started to panic. She was standing beside me, almost touching my right arm with her left. I heard her gasp and then I heard her curse. Out of the corner of my eye, I saw her arms go up in a protective movement and before I could fully turn toward her she started to flail away at the few bees around us. I immediately turned, grabbed her in a full body hug pulling her arms down by her side and holding them there as I pushed her to the ground and fell on top of her. The momentum of my push took us off the path and we landed on some rocks and near some cactus. Her cheek struck a rock and was cut by its sharp edge and she yelled out in pain and pushed against me in protest; but I held tight, and as we slid down the slight rocky incline, we also slid over the cactus. The cactus spines ripped into our legs and backs but did not cause any serious injury. We did not stop sliding until we reached the bottom of the incline. Once we reached the bottom I tilted her face so that she was looking directly into my eyes. I then smiled and told her that everything was going to be fine and that I wanted her to keep her eyes closed until I told her to open them. Then I pressed my body tight against hers, and we waited. As we waited, I spoke quietly to her, hoping to help her regain the mastery of self-control that is so much a part of her personality. The bees had started to sting me and I knew we were still in serious peril. We had to remain calm, because if we behaved aggressively, then it could be fatal to us both. I am not afraid of dying as it happens to all of us eventually, but I do not want to die of food poisoning and I do not want to die from bee stings. Death by food poisoning seems such a wasteful way to die and I do not want to die that way. Death by bee stings seemed imminently possible and I was not ready to go just yet. The bees were still buzzing around us but they were not swarming. However, many of them had landed on the exposed skin of my arms and face and I could feel their stings burning my skin like fire. I could not see my legs, but I knew there were bees on them as well because I could feel their sting through my jeans. I opened my eyes just enough to look at her and I could see that there were a few dozen bees on her as well. Although she was not fighting me, I knew that she was getting stung. I whispered to her to keep her eyes closed and everything would be just fine. I felt her head nod, indicating that she had heard me and that she understood. Then she started to softly cry. As I lay there trying to remain calm and make an rational assessment of our situation, I realized with horror that I could feel bees stinging my ankles and I knew that they had gotten under my jean cuffs and into my boots. My heart sank and I tried not to panic as I next felt bees crawling on my scalp and down my shirt color. There were bees stinging the fleshy area just behind my ears and there were bees crawling in my ear, their noise temporarily drowning out the noise of those buzzing around me. I closed my eyes even tighter and said a silent prayer as I felt a few bees crawling over my lips and tickling my nose as they probed my nostrils. I wanted to whisper to her once more but I was afraid to open my lips. I did pull her closer to me.

I lost all track of time as we lay there not moving for what seemed like an eternity. When I did eventually open my eyes, I could see that there were not as many bees on us as before. They had left us and re-joined the ones flying around and above us, still on alert but no longer on attack. I could feel her body start to relax as she gained back her self-control and I eased up on the bear hug I had her in. We lay there unmoving for another several minutes. The vibration of the hive was incredible in the sheer force of the power it emitted, and we realized how lucky we had been so far. The number of bees interested in us declined steadily and after another several minutes we stood up and slowly retraced our steps back the way we had come. The cut on her face had almost stopped bleeding. I think it was because the dried blood had sealed the wound and stopped any fresh blood from seeping out. I looked at her and said, "That will leave a scar."

"Yes, thanks for noticing." She said. Then she stopped and looked directly into my eyes and embarrassingly said, "I also want to thank you for also saving my life back there. I lost control of myself and I did start to panic. If you had not grabbed me, I was going to run, and if I had run then I would have probably gotten us both killed. I am sorry for losing control and thank you for helping me get it back. It will not happen again."

"You're welcome," was the only reply I could make. I could feel my body start to shake as the stress began to fall away. We really escaped a tight one and I did not realize how afraid I had been until now that it was over. Trying to be humorous I continued, "It is funny that my knee no longer hurts where you banged it with the jeep door, but these cactus pricks and these bee stings are sure painful." Neither of us laughed.

We continued walking and limping back down the path, past the shack, and arrived back at the jeep without incident. This entire experience took place within less than a mile and in just over 90 minutes. It was an approximately 3/4 of a mile roundtrip from the jeep to the spot where we encountered the bees and we were both really thirsty when we arrived back at the jeep. She started to open a fresh canteen of water but stopped herself. It would be best if we did not open any water containers until we were in the jeep and at least several miles further away. We just escaped a horde of bees and we did not want to now attract them back with water. Needless to say, that I had no intention of obeying any posted speed limit in covering those miles.

I got in behind the wheel as she settled into the passenger seat. "Now, how about we start driving again and see if we can figure out where we are," I said more to myself than to her.

5

We did not drive that far but we once again drove in silence. The realization of how fortunate we had been to escape those bees with just the injuries we suffered was beginning to sink in. We read about that sort of thing happening but you never really fully understand the terror of a bee attack until it happens to you. There is absolutely no escape when you are out in the open like we were.

I still had no clear idea of where we were, so as I drove, I looked for a road sign that would give me a clue, or even a gas station where I could stop and ask directions.

She spent the time cleaning the cut on her face using tissues and water from the canteen. Now that it was cleaned up it did not look as bad as it had looked back there on the path, but we both knew that it would leave a mark on her cheek. The thing that was bothering both of us the most was not the cut on her face, or my slightly swollen knee cap, or the bee stings, or even the fact that we were lost; it was the exhaustion we both felt. Once the adrenaline rush, caused by a potentially life-threatening situation, subsides and the brain starts to process what has happened, the experience can leave the body exhausted of its energy reserves. We both felt this but knew we needed to find out where we were and get some help.

We only drove 15 minutes or so but it was late afternoon, around 4:30pm, when I pulled off of the road and onto an unkempt gravel driveway. I drove about 40 yards up this driveway until I reached the edge of a deep, washed out area that cut right though the center of the driveway and prevented me from driving any further. I parked the jeep and stopped the engine as we both sat and stared at the farm house. The house sat at the end of what was now more of a worn path than a real driveway and it was about 40 yards further up the driveway on the other side of the washed out area. The house sat in the midst of what at one time was a very large field of some type of crop; probably corn, or cotton, or roses. Now it was just uncultivated land that had been neglected for quite some time and gone to seed. The driveway itself ran through the field and along the top of a dirt embankment that was just a little higher than the surrounding field. Each side of the driveway gently sloped downward to the field, and along each side, these huge old palm trees grew in a line that stretched from the road to the house. There was one tree approximately every 30 feet on each side of the driveway so that the trees ran parallel to the driveway on each side. The driveway ended at the overgrown side yard on the left of the house as we stood facing it. The palm trees on the left side of the driveway continued until they had passed the house and reached the end boundary of the backyard at which point they turned right. The palm trees on the right of the driveway turned right where they met the also overgrown front yard. Then they ran along the edge of the front yard until they reached the boundary on the front side of the house, at which point they turned left. Thus, the entire line of palm trees on each side of the driveway eventually met and formed what was one long continuous line of trees that began at the road and then bordered and encircled not only the driveway but the house as well. I imagined that if viewed from above, the palm trees around the property would look like a giant capital letter P with the house right in the middle of the enclosed part of the letter. It was obvious that at one time this had been a very prosperous farm that had quite a showcase entrance. It was equally obvious that someone had put a lot of time, pride and thought into designing and building it. However, it was now sadly obvious that no pride and no effort had been put into maintaining either the trees or the driveway in quite some time. The driveway was pitted and eroded and a vehicle would have difficulty reaching the house from the road. In addition, the palm fronds and bark on the trees showed their age and neglect as well. The fronds were mostly dead and had turned brown and were hanging down the sides of the trees like loose and broken wallpaper.

The house itself was a compact adobe rancher with a porch that appeared to wrap around the entire house. At the very least, the porch ran along the front of the house and also along the side of the house that we could see. The porch was also framed with a white washed wood railing that added a certain charm that I thought looked out of place. Large picture windows branched off on either side of the faded red entry door which was located right in the middle of the front of the house. All of the windows appeared to be intact and dirty, but not broken; so I assumed someone still lived in the house. There was a red brick chimney at each end of the house, which indicated the probable location of the bedrooms and there was also one red brick double chimney in the middle of the house that probably marked the living room or den. The house itself was the color of cigarette ash. It was not a color that had been chosen and then painted. It was a color that had evolved from whatever the original color had been and was the result of years of bleaching by the sun, washing by the rain, blasting by the sand, and drying by the wind. In other words, it was a color that was also the result of neglect. The roof appeared to be made of wooden cedar shingles which had dried and curled and were missing in places. These were also the color of ash, but interspersed with random spotted areas that were darker in color.

We sat in the parked jeep for several minutes, studying the house and looking for any sign of movement or even habitation. We were hoping that we could find someone at home here that could tell us where we were and could also give us directions. We could also use some minor first aid treatment for our injuries and some gas for the jeep. Something to eat would be nice too, but we would not ask for that. However, we would accept it if it were offered.

After a few more moments she said, "If any people are in that house, they may be watching us watch them. Since this is their property, and we are a strange vehicle with strangers in it parked on their land, and we have done nothing but sit here and study their house, then it is possible they could be getting a little suspicious of our intentions."

"Excellent point," I mumbled. We then discussed whether we should leave our guns in the car but quickly decided against that for a couple of reasons. The first obvious one is that we did not know who lived there. It could be drug dealers or it could be a drop house for illegals and neither of those would exactly be friendly. The second reason we decided to keep our guns is because even if the house was inhabited by a helpful person, this is still Arizona and it is not unusual for people to carry guns.

We each exited the jeep so that it would be clear that there were only the two of us. We stood there for a few moments listening for any sound that came from the house but it was absolutely silent. Other than a hawk hunting field mice on one side of the field and a couple of buzzards circling out over the other side of the field, nothing stirred around us. There was no breeze to rustle the palm fronds, no birds singing, no crickets chirping, no dogs barking, and no bees. I don't know how to describe it other than there was just utter and complete silence.

A soft whistle from her broke the silence. Just slightly turning her head towards me, but not taking her eyes off of the house, she said, "We are not alone. I think I can see someone sitting in a chair on the porch to the left of the entry door. If you look about halfway between the picture window and the door you may be able to see what I am talking about. I can just make out what appears to be a head just above the porch rail and also what looks to be a boot propped up on the rail as well."

I followed her gaze with my eyes and said, "Yes, I see what you are talking about. Sure looks like a head and a foot to me as well."

"Hey there!," I yelled.

No response.

We took a few more steps forward, stopped, and yelled again. This time we saw movement. The person leaned forward and the head rose up as if to look over the railing. Strangely, the boot on the railing did not move, but now we knew that we had been looking at a man's head and we waited to see what he would do. He did not speak or call out to us. He did not even stand up. After a few moments, he simply raised his right arm above his head and motioned for us to come on up. The movement of his arm was fluid, but it was slow and appeared to be restricted. The way he waved his arm was more of a wave that began at the elbow and ended at the wrist instead of a wave that began from the shoulder and involved the whole arm. I got the impression that it was a much older man that we were about to meet.

With the exception of disturbing a few ant hills, the remaining walk from the jeep to the front porch was uneventful. We walked through the knee high overgrown and unkempt scrub brush that made up the front yard in silence, moving our eyes from the rough and tangled ground upon which we walked up to the porch where the man we were about to meet sat motionless. There were five stone steps leading up to the wooden plank floor of the front porch, and as we reached the landing we were greeted by a strong and friendly voice. Without standing or moving to greet us, he simply said, "Welcome, strangers." He paused for just a second and then continued, "My name is Clement but usually folks just call me Clem. At least, that is what folks used to call me when folks used to come over. You probably cannot tell by looking at the place, but I have not had company come over to visit in a long time. However, since you are folks and since you have come over, you may as well call me Clem. How long have you been sitting there in the driveway like that? I had fallen asleep and was dreaming about the most beautiful naked woman and her also naked sister and I did not hear anything until you started yelling at me like some damn fool. Woke me up and scared away the dream too. Damn shame as I cannot remember the last time I saw a woman naked and there I was dreaming about two of them." He made a noise clearing his throat that implied he was finished talking and then actually looked at us for the first time.

He appeared to be in his mid-80s. His face was lean and clean shaven with a strong jaw and thin lips. He had a full head of hair that reminded me of the yard we had just walked through, dry and unkempt. His eyes were large and overly liquid. The pupils were an indistinguishable color of light brown and dark green and almost translucent. They reminded me of eyes I had seen many times before in old men. Eyes that reflected back at you instead of letting you in. Eyes that almost hurt to look at and I found myself intentionally diverting my gaze only to have it drawn right back. They were tired eyes that been exposed to too much wind and sun. His were eyes that knew and understood many lessons, but gave no hint that the man behind the eyes wanted to talk about them. It was difficult to tell exactly where he was looking and I noticed that his stare was more in my general direction instead of directly at me. I thought maybe he had cataracts and I wondered at just how well he could see. His expression was a mixture of friendliness and curiosity. It was only when he reached for the crutch that lay on the floor next to his chair that I noticed he only had one leg. He was dressed in what looked to be a comfortable well-worn white cotton shirt and faded blue jeans. The right blue jean pant leg that would have held the missing appendage was neatly folded back just above where the knee would have been and sewn shut. His one foot was barefoot. Now I understood why the boot on the railing did not move when he leaned forward.

Propping the crutch under his right arm, he hoisted himself up to a full standing position. Seeming satisfied that we were all now on pretty much the same level and no one was looking down at him, he turned his watery gaze to her and asked, "What can I get you drink, pretty lady?" Before she could answer, he said, "I can give you anything at all that you want to drink as long as it is either water or coffee." You see, it was a promise to my wife to only offer guests water or coffee."

"Where is your wife now?" she asked.

"In the graveyard," he said. "It was my drinking that killed her and it was my drinking that also took my leg. I'll show you her grave later on if you'd like to see it. My leg is buried next to her in what should one day be my grave, but for now, all it holds is the remains of my leg. Since my drinking took both my leg and my wife from me, it seemed altogether fitting and proper that they should be buried next to each other." Then with a smile, he finished by saying, "I thought about having my leg buried with her in the same coffin, but then the problem arose of where in relation to her body should my leg be in the coffin. I did not want my foot in her face but I also did not want the stump of my thigh in her face. When I could not find an answer that did not seem disrespectful to either her or my leg, I just had my leg buried separately."

She gave him a funny look as if she was not sure if he was kidding or serious. I could see on her face that she was trying to decide. Several seconds passed, and then after making up her mind as to which it was she asked, "Don't you want to know our names or why we are here?"

"Nope," he said. "Don't care. What difference does it make if I know your names or not? What guarantee do I have that the names you tell me would be your true names anyway? And I assume you are here because you are lost." He then gave each of us a quick once over glance before continuing, "And from the looks of you I'd say that you could use a little doctoring up as well." He turned his gaze to me and gave me a look of reprimand for her dirty clothes, the cut on her cheek, the bee sting marks, and the other scratches from the cactus she had. He did not seem to notice or care that I had a few injuries as well. "Now, what can I get you to drink?"

I wanted to say that the real reason we were there was because we had turned left instead of right back at that T intersection a few hours ago and that we had made that left turn only because that is what she had wanted to do. I knew that if we had chosen to turn right like I had wanted to do, that we would not be here. I don't know where we would be, but I did know that it would not be here. Upon further consideration, I saw no advantage in bringing that subject up again.

We both asked for coffee, black with no sweetener. With the instructions memorized, he opened the red wooden front door and crutch-stepped over the threshold into his house. She and I looked at each other for a moment, shrugged our shoulders, and followed him inside.

6

Stepping across the threshold into the front room was like taking a step back in time. The front door opened into a room that would have been appropriate in an 1880's ranch home in the Southwest. Clem moved on ahead of us as she and I stood there in awe. The windows were covered with heavy drapes that were made of blue and gold fabric and bordered in red trim. These drapes had been pulled almost completely closed. There was no electrical source of light that was obvious; all lighting that we could see was gas, oil, or candle. Steer hides served as rugs and these were scattered across the hand hewn planked wooden floor. The plaster walls were covered with old portraits which I assumed were of family, a couple of old hand wound pendulum clocks, and a large mirror in a gilded frame. The furnishings were old and consisted of a few well-worn dark red leather chairs, several fine wooden tables, two overstuffed sofas, a side boy, and barrister style book cases that lined one wall. However, everything was in surprisingly excellent shape given the condition of the exterior of the house and grounds. The oil lamps on the tables and the oil chandelier suspended by a chain from the ceiling cast pools of light and shadow that was both pleasing and welcoming. There was an unlit large stone fireplace against the back wall with a massive wooden mantel running the length of the stone wall. Groups of relatively new and distinctly antique firearms were hanging from pegs above the mantel piece. The feeling of the room was that of a library or a reading room in an upper class men's club. Everything was placed to give a refined, comfortable, and welcoming feeling. I had a brief thought of how appropriate it would be to settle down into one of those chairs and call the butler to bring me a book, a glass of scotch, and a cigar.

This time my thoughts were interrupted by Clem. He was speaking to her and pointing off towards the other side of the room, "Just go down this hallway over here, the first room on the right is a bathroom. There is a first aid kit in the cabinet under the sink." Looking her up and down, he continued, "You may want to take a bath or a shower first and clean those injuries up a bit before you put medicine on them though. You'll find some towels in the cabinet as well. I have some extra clothes that belong to my daughter-in-law that may fit you. I will set them outside the bathroom door and you can change into them when you are done. Then I will show you where the washing machine is and you can wear her clothes while yours are in the wash."

"Thanks," she said. "I do have a change of clothes in the jeep but I am tired and sore and I really do not feel like unpacking them right now, so I will take you up on your offer to borrow your daughter-in-law's."

When she was on her way to the bathroom he turned to me and said, "You look like you could use some first aid too. You have quite a few bee stings and they can get infected if you don't take care of them. It also looks like you both got tangled up with some cactus. After she finishes taking care of herself, you should go wash and do some doctoring to your injuries too. You can tell me what happened later if you care to."

Then he looked at me and asked, "So what will it be, coffee or water?" Apparently he had already forgotten our request, so I repeated that we would both like some black coffee with no sweetener. I also added that a couple of glasses of water would be welcomed too. Once he had this order, he disappeared through an arched doorway to the right of the fireplace that I assumed led into the kitchen.

He popped his head back around the corner a few seconds later and said, "I'll have to brew the coffee which will take a few minutes. Feel free to look around and make yourself at home."

"Thanks," I said. Then just as he was about to disappear back into the kitchen I thought to ask him a question. "Do you have a phone we could use?"

A slight frown crossed his face and then he replied, "No, I have not had one of those in years. We, my wife and I, used to have one on what you probably refer to now-a-days as a land line. We had it mounted on the kitchen wall right by the stove. The phone was avocado green and the numbers, which were on the receiver instead of the base of the phone, would glow in the dark. It also had a 30 foot cord that attached the receiver to the phone base so that my wife could talk and move about the kitchen at the same time. The cord was long enough that she could even do laundry and talk on it. She was tickled by that and she thought it was the best invention ever. I hated that cord however. It was always in the way or it would get tangled up with itself. I had it disconnected shortly after she died and I have not had a reason to have one since."

"Great," I thought to myself as I stood there taking in the room. I could hear the shower running from the bathroom down the hall and I knew she had accepted his offer of washing off. I could also hear him opening and closing cabinet doors back in the kitchen area. Realizing that I was really alone in the room and being curious I walked over to the wall that was lined with the barrister book cases. Upon closer examination, I could see that they were not one long continuous bookcase, which was my first impression upon entering the room. They were rather a series of perfectly matched yet individual book cases placed side by side. These stretched along the length of the entire wall. Each case was a little over 3 feet tall and 4 feet wide with one built in shelf. The bottom of each case also served as an additional shelf. These small cases were anchored at each end by matching cases that were at least 6 feet tall. The front of each of the smaller bookcase consisted of two panes of glass; each pane was enclosed in its own wooden frame. The taller book cases had 6 panes each. On all of the bookcases, each of these panes was separately hinged along the top so that the pane could be lifted and swung outward and upward. Then once opened, the pane of glass was lined up with track rails so that it could be slid back into the bookcase and out of the way. The result was that the glass served not only as a protective barrier to the contents, but also as a way to get into the bookcase. These glass panes were well polished and crystal clear. The cases themselves were packed full with books and old newspapers and also with what appeared to be Indian artifacts, miner artifacts, small photos in frames, and some cloth badges that appeared to be from England or Scotland. The effect was impressive.

"I would be more than happy to open those cases for you if there is something in particular that you would like to see," he said as he re-entered the room with 3 glasses filled with water and ice on a silver tray. In addition to the water glasses, there was a sterling silver coffee pot on the tray. The pot had an engraving of what looked like a family crest or coat of arms. He sat it down on the coffee table between the two sofas. Before I could respond, he asked me to follow him. I noticed that Clem got around pretty well for an old man on a crutch and only one leg, but there was only so much he can carry and he was a bit out of practice at entertaining. He disappeared again through the arched doorway and I followed him into the kitchen. It was a functional but unremarkable kitchen. There was a door at the far end of the kitchen which was closed. There was also another door that led outside to the rear of the house. I could see that the porch and the railing looked the same as the front, so my initial guess that it was a wrap-around porch appeared to be correct. The counter tops were covered with light gray Formica and the floor was yellow linoleum and was cracked in spots. The cabinets were white and hung from plaster walls; the walls were faded and were just a few shades darker than the cabinets. Everything in the room needed an update. The color of the stove and oven was harvest gold and both were gas; but I noticed that the old white refrigerator was electric, as was the single light bulb hanging from the ceiling. I made a mental note to ask him about the electricity in this room later. Overall, everything was old but very clean.

He saw me looking around and I could tell he was a little embarrassed. He said, "I apologize for how out of date everything must look to you. My wife and I had plans to remodel the kitchen but just never got around to it. Then there really seemed no point to doing it after she died. The door that is closed leads to a short hallway where there is a small laundry room. Then, my bedroom and bathroom are just past that. The other door leads out to the back yard." He then pointed to another silver tray that held three fine porcelain coffee cups and saucers along with intricately carved matching sterling silver serving trees that held a selection of miniature cheese sandwiches and icing covered finger cakes at the end of each limb. He asked if I would grab that tray while he filled a pitcher with ice and water. We brought these items back out and sat them down on the coffee table next to the glasses and coffee pot.

She entered the room at this time and sat down in one of the leather chairs without saying a word. She looked at the refreshments that Clem had sat out and then she looked at him. With a slight smile she said, "Thanks Clem, these look delicious and the setting is beautiful. I also want to say thanks for the shower and the medicine and the clean clothes. If you will show me where your washer is, then I will take care of washing my clothes so that you can have these back." Her hair was partially wet and hung down over her eyes a little. She had a bandage on the cut on her cheek and I could see the dried residue of where she had put some type of ointment on the bee stings. She looked very tired, with dark circles under each eye, but she also looked like she felt a great deal better. It is amazing what a little soap and water and some clean clothes will do to perk a person up after a difficult day.

Clem grinned like a school boy at these expressions of gratitude from her and responded with, "You are welcome honey. We'll take care of the washing soon enough. You just sit right there and relax and have something to eat and drink. Those clothes look like they fit you pretty well. I thought you were about the same size as Elizabeth, my daughter-in-law. I may be old but I am glad that I still have the ability to size up a woman's figure, especially one as nice as yours."

She blushed and smiled at that.

I just rolled my eyes.

As he poured the coffee, she reached for a clover shaped cake with green icing. I reached for diamond shaped cake with pink icing.

"That was an interesting choice," he said to me.

"Why do you say that?" I asked.

"Because you do not look like a man who would choose pink," he responded.

"Oh, pink is my favorite color," I said. It reminds me of one of my favorite things."

He gave a snort, looked at me and winked, and then gave me a nudge in my ribs the way old men will do.

She was looking around the room, examining the décor, and pretending not to hear Clem and me. "This is a very interesting room" she finally said.

"Thank you," he replied. "I refer to it as the family room because it holds family memories for me. This house only has a few other rooms. "As you may have already guessed," then he briefly looked at me and continued, "and as you already know, the kitchen is behind the wall with the fireplace and through that arched door way. From the kitchen, there is access to the laundry, my bedroom, and bathroom which is behind the kitchen. It was the garage originally, but my wife and I converted it into our bedroom and bathroom after our 2nd son was born." Then he turned his gaze on her and continued, "And, as you now know, to the right as you enter this room is a hallway that connects to the bathroom that you just used. Further down that hallway are two bedrooms that were where our sons slept when they were little and lived here. Once they were grown, they would stay in those rooms when they came to visit."

"If you don't mind me asking, what is the deal with the family crest on the coffee pot and all the artifacts and badges in the book cases?" I asked.

"It is a coat of arms on the coffee pot," he replied. "It is not a family crest. Although the two terms are used interchangeably, there is a difference, and that is something we can discuss later. Most of these things in the book cases are heirlooms. My ancestors were large land owners in England and owned over 50,000 acres of land in the north of England, right around the border with Scotland. These land holdings began as a grant of a few thousand acres to my ancestors during the reign of the House of Stewart just after the Union of the Crowns. Over the generations, my ancestors added to this grant and eventually there were several large estates and other smaller houses on this land as well. Over time, they became extremely wealthy. So wealthy, in fact, that by the time my great-great grandfather was born no one in the family needed to work. They lived off of the income they received from the farming tenants who lived on and cultivated their enormous land holdings. They were also fortunate that some of their lands contained rich seams of coal for mining, which added to the fortune. As a young man, all my great-great grandfather had to occupy himself with was spending his days hunting and running his dogs, and his nights socializing with people just like him. On those days when he was not hunting, he spent his time travelling or improving his acreage in England by adding deer parks and gardens and making upgrades to his multiple beautiful homes."

"Must have been quite a life," she said.

"Yes, but it gets better," he said. "These ancestors were born into a privileged life and took it as a matter of course that people would defer to them just because of their class or status. So, it was quite a shock to my great-great grandfather and his friends when they came to America in 1846 to hunt buffalo. He could not grasp the concept that class did not matter here and the whole 'all men are created equal' frame of mind. The people he met on the western frontier straightened him out right quick. While I don't think he ever fully understood the concept, he did come to respect it."

"Wait, your great-great grandfather came all the way from England to America just to hunt buffalo?" she asked.

"Not exactly, but that was one of the main reasons he came over. Our family already had several branches that had been in America for generations. These relations had all settled in Virginia and the Carolinas and, with few exceptions, had stayed 'back East'. I really do not know that much about most of them. My great-great-grandfather had a different experience and I think it is an interesting story but I am not sure you will think so or if you even want to hear it. I am pretty sure that the only reason you are here is because you are lost. It is not a very long story, but if you need to be on your way, I understand."

She looked at me with no expression at all on her face. I returned the look and the expression. After a moment of silence, where neither of us broke eye contact, she said "I'd like to hear the story."

"Ok, me too," I responded.

"Wonderful!" he said. "I do not have company over much anymore and this is quite a treat for me. If you get hungry, you know where the kitchen is and please make yourselves at home. I live here alone, so there is nothing special to eat. However, if you care to look, there are canned goods in the cabinets and in the pantry, and there is some meat in the freezer. The pots and pans and other cooking utensils are under the counter to the right of the stove and there are some other leftovers in the fridge. The house does have electricity and every room has lights and air conditioning, I just prefer not to use electric light in this family room."

I erased the mental note I had made to ask him about the electric light and refrigerator that I had seen in the kitchen.

"You two can get around easier than I can, so if you want something just help yourself. And you also know that the bathrooms are just down that hallway if you need to visit those."

"Mind if I smoke?" I asked.

"Not at all," he said. "There is an ashtray and matches up on the mantel and some others scattered around."

"That is ok," I said. "I don't smoke. I was only curious to see just how far your accommodating hospitality would go. I see that it appears to have no limit."

"Oh," he said with a tone and a look that could have turned a warm spring rain drop into a cold winter cube of ice. After a moment, he gathered himself and smiled as he looked at me. "You have an odd sense of humor and fortunately, I like that."

He paused for a few seconds and stared at me with those reflective liquid brown eyes. Just as the silence was getting uncomfortable, he continued. "You have no idea how far my hospitality may extend, but you will find out if you stay long enough."

Now it was her turn to freeze me with an even colder look as she excused herself and got up to go use the bathroom. I cleared my throat and poured myself another cup of coffee.

Once we had refreshed ourselves, Clem continued.

"Before I start this story, I think it would be best if the two of you stayed here for the night. It is already half past 6 and even though you are not that far from a town, I can tell you have both had a long day."

She agreed right away to his offer, which settled the matter without the need for us to have to have a conversation about it.

"Ok, thanks Clem," I said. "We are pretty beat and that is very generous of you to offer. I think I will take you up on that shower and medicine now too if you don't mind. Can you wait until I return to start your story?"

"Yes sirree, no problem pard," he said. "Be sure to take special care of those stings. I am afraid I don't have any clothes that will fit you but there is a bathrobe I can provide for you to wear until your clothes are washed."

She stood at this time and said, "Leave your clothes outside the bathroom door and I will start our laundry while you are in the shower."

I started towards the hallway and the bathroom but stopped and turned and asked Clem, "Just where are we anyway? You mentioned that we are not that far from a town."

"Correct," he replied. "You cannot see it from here, but if you turn left at the end of the driveway onto the main road and then drive just a couple of miles you will be able to see Vulture Peak in the distance to the north. It is about an hour's drive from here and then the town of Wickenburg is just a few miles further east from that landmark. The only thing between here and Wickenburg is a couple more ranch houses and a country store. Then, from Wickenburg, you can take the 60 highway east towards Phoenix, or you can take highway 93 north which will take you towards Las Vegas, or you can go west through pretty much nothing but desert until you come to the Lake Havasu area."

He paused for a second and then asked, "Which way did you come in?"

"Thanks, Clem," I said. "We came in from the opposite direction. We got lost a few miles back at a T intersection and I was not really sure where we were, but now I have a pretty good idea."

"Oh yes, I know that intersection" he said. "In order to get here, you drove right past an old mine that one of my ancestors worked a long time ago, back in the day when people would come here to stake a claim and prospect for gold and silver. I forget exactly what the relationship of that ancestor is, a distant something or another. He belonged to those 'back East' ancestors that I mentioned earlier; I think this one was a 4th or 5th cousin. I do remember some things about him though from the stories my mama and daddy used to tell. His name was Cyrus and the mine itself is 15 or 20 minutes from here. It never was a very productive mine, and although it is still family property, it was abandoned long ago. I think it is sealed up now, but I am not sure as I have not been up to look at it in years. Anyway, family legend has it that Cyrus was half crazy and pretty much stayed to himself. He hailed from Virginia where he was a loner and no'er-do-well. When the war came, he was one of the first to join the Southern States in their battle for independence during the "Late Unpleasantness" or the "War of Northern Aggression" as my parents called it. It is more widely known as the Civil War. He served in The Army of Northern Virginia for the entire war. He was in every major infantry battle fought on Virginia soil, plus he was at Antietam in Maryland and Gettysburg in Pennsylvania. He must have been very lucky but his battle exploits are unknown and probably unremarkable. He was just an ordinary soldier, one of hundreds of thousands. He was wounded in the leg somewhere near Petersburg, during the siege of that city near the war's end, and captured by the Yankees. After the war, he was paroled but remained an 'Un-Reconstructed Rebel'. He was constantly in and out of trouble with the Union authorities and chafed at their occupation of Virginia. He eventually drifted west and ended up here in Arizona. He did some gambling and took up mining, and after a while, staked his own claim; that would have been around 1868. He was not well known and not well liked, but he managed to avoid trouble by staying to himself and working his claim. However, only four or five years had to pass before trouble came to him again. He was accused of raping a missionary woman and killing her husband. The missionaries were headed up north to the Grand Canyon area to civilize and save the souls of some Navahos. Anyway, these missionaries stopped near Cyrus's claim to camp for the night. The woman was found wandering the desert half dead a few days later by a passing stagecoach and she told them what had happened. No one really knows what happened to my cousin. One story is that a territorial Marshall came out with a group of men and hanged him. Another story is that he ran off and was either killed by Indians or died in the desert. You see, no records were kept on men like him back then. He simply disappeared."

"I used to ride my horse up to the old claim and explore the mine and the ruins of his shack when I was a boy. There is an artifact that I found near the ruins of his old shack and I put it in that tall cabinet by the window. I found it one day when I was up at the mine exploring. However, I did not find this artifact at the mine; I found it at the shack. It was inside the walls, right where the door would have been. I threw a rock at a lizard that was sunning itself, and when I did so, the lizard ran into its hole. When it did that, it disturbed some trash by the door and I got a glimpse of something shiny reflected in the sun. When I went to investigate, I found an Indian Head penny dated 1869. But that is not what was shiny, the penny just happened to be lying next to it. I pulled the shiny thing out of the dirt and saw that it had his name scratched into the back of it, and that is how I am pretty sure it was his. It was the only thing ever found that could be at least proven by association to have once belonged to him."

I walked over to the bookcase to take a look and asked which artifact he meant.

"On the top shelf, the tin spoon with the small piece of rope tied to it," he said. "Some miners would tie their spoons to a stationary object when they were not in use, so that animals or birds would not carry them away. The birds and animals were attracted by shiny objects, and spoons were just the right size to easily hijack."

I looked up at the spoon and the vision of the old miner that I had seen at the mine shack earlier in the day came back to me. I mumbled, "Yes, I met Cyrus at the mine."

"Beg pardon?" He asked. "I did not hear what you said. Could you repeat it please?"

"I said, I know where that mine is." Then, turning towards him, I continued, "Daisy and I saw that mine and what remains of your cousin's shack today. The mine is where we had the encounter with the bees. I don't think the mine is sealed because the bees appear to have built a hive in it. If the mine is sealed, then it is not sealed very well. All that remains of the shack is some rubble, but the walls are still standing."

And with that, I headed off to the shower. As I turned the corner to go down the hall, I heard him say to her, "Daisy, huh?" Well, it just figures you would be named after my favorite flower. I think the daisy is the prettiest flower there is and it is an appropriate name for you honey."

I heard her laugh and thank him for the compliment. I knew she was probably smiling at him and blushing too. I just shook my head and rolled my eyes for the second time in less than an hour that day.

I stripped and dropped my dirty clothes outside the door to the bathroom and then I took what felt at the time to be the best shower of my life. The water stung when it first hit the bee stings and the spots where the cactus spines had stuck me. I had forgotten that this part might be painful and I was surprised at the pain. I involuntarily jumped back to escape the water and banged my still aching knee against the shower door in doing so. So, I re-evaluated my approach and eased myself under the water spray on the next try. It hurt some initially, but both injury types felt immensely better after I bathed them using a wash cloth lathered up with lots of soap and warm water. It became one of those things for which there is a saying that goes something like "it hurt so bad that it felt good", and I did not want to get out.

Eventually, I did reluctantly get out of the shower. I opened the bathroom door and found that my old dirty clothes had been replaced by a royal blue terry cloth robe and white slippers. I retrieved both of these items, finished liberally dabbing some antibiotic cream on my stings and scrapes, and then exited the bathroom and headed back down the hall towards the living room. I heard Clem call my name and I turned around to see him standing inside the doorway to one of the two bedrooms that shared this hall with the bathroom.

"Feeling better?" he asked. "You sure look like you have re-joined the land of the living as you were looking pretty peaked earlier."

"Oh yeah, much better," I replied. "We really appreciate everything you have done for us to make us feel comfortable."

"You are welcome; it is a treat for me to have you here. Like I said earlier, I don't get company any longer and I don't get out much other than an occasional trip to the market once a month or so to get the basics. I have an old Chevy pickup that I use to drive the 25 minutes it takes to get to the market and usually I don't see anyone other than the kid who works the place. I know his name only because it is on his nametag, but he hardly even notices me. He is too busy playing with his phone to have any conversation with a customer. All he does is ring up my purchases on the old register and mumble what could barely pass as a 'thanks" as he bags my goods. He does help carry my bags to the truck though, but he never talks. It is my habit, learned the hard way, to always pay cash; so I am sure he does not have any idea of my name or where I live. Anyway, I am glad you are feeling better. Daisy is doing the wash and I thought I would setup these rooms for you two. Both are ready and you all can use whichever one you want or both."

He and I walked back down the hallway together and met her coming around the corner from the family room, with freshly washed and folded laundry in her arms.

"Well, you certainly look like you are getting comfortable" she said looking at me. "If I did not know better, I would think you were on vacation in some swanky resort dressed like that." She continued before I could respond, "I am just going to lay these clean things out for you and I am also going to change back into my own clothes. Then I will join you boys in the family room to hear the beginning of Clem's story." She paused for a moment and then continued, "No offense meant Clem, as I am sure your story will be fascinating, but it has been a long day and I am not sure how long I will be able to keep my eyes open this evening."

"No problem, honey," he replied. "We can talk as long as you want tonight and then we can always take up tomorrow where we leave off tonight."

"Thanks, you are a sweetheart Clem." Then, looking at me, she said, "I cleaned your gun up a bit while you were in the shower. It is lying on the coffee table alongside your belt. I also walked out to the jeep and pulled it around back, outside the shed where Clem parks. He showed me the path he takes when he goes out in his pickup and I was able to get the jeep around back without a problem."

"Thank you for doing all of that," I replied. "My gun got quite dirty from that fall that you and I took back at the bee mine, and I feel better knowing that the jeep is around back instead of down near the road." I then continued, "But since I am dressed for vacation, I think I will leave the gun and gun belt off for the rest of the evening. Besides, this bathrobe is quite comfortable but it does not have any belt loops strong enough to hold up the gun belt."

Clem and I left her to change and headed back to the family room where we each took a seat in a red leather chair. I sank into it like it was butter.

He leaned over and asked, "What is the relationship between the two of you, if you don't mind me asking?"

"Well, Clem," I began, "That is a darn good question, and damn if I know the answer. It is complex and it is complicated and it changes constantly. I will promise to tell you if and when I figure it out."

He leaned back and loudly laughed. Once he regained himself he said, "I remember that feeling well, Colonel. It was that way with almost every woman I ever knew, including my late wife. Good rest her soul. It is just our fate as men that we have to keep trying to figure out the game when the women never tell us the rules."

He leaned back and winked at me before continuing, "It is a fun game though." Then he sighed and added with a wistful smile, "At least when you are still young enough to play it. Women are strange creatures you know. Most of them are all about love and providing comfort to those that they love. They also want to feel loved and made to feel like they are special and valued. Some women have more of it to give than others, but basically, it is love they want. Men want love too but I don't think to the same extent as a woman. Sure, some men need more than others and I think there are some who don't need any love at all and are incapable of giving any. Those are the ones to stay away from. I think the trick to a man and a woman finding happiness is that a man needs to understand that a woman needs to give and receive love, and the woman needs to understand that a man feels differently about love. The key is for the man and the woman to find that balance in each other. If that can be done, then happiness will follow." He paused for a moment as if he was reflecting on what he had just said. A moment later, he sighed and simply said, "I am far from an expert on this, but that is at least the opinion of this old man."

"Well, I certainly appreciate that insight and point of view. I had never thought of it like that before and now some things that have happened make sense. I am open to any other wisdom you care to share," I said. Then I asked, "Why did you call me Colonel, just now?"

"No real reason. I just figured that since I don't know your name and really do not want to know it, that I would just give you a title and call you by that," he said.

"Makes sense," I replied, "but if want to call me by a title, then how about calling me Doc instead of Colonel"?

"Are you a doctor?" he asked.

"Nope," I replied.

"Well, ok. Is there any special reason you prefer Doc over Colonel?" he asked.

"Of course," I replied. "There is a reason for everything, but it is a long story and we already have one long story ahead of us tonight."

We were then interrupted as she walked in the room and joined us by quietly taking a seat on one of the overstuffed couches. We watched her for a few minutes as she rearranged every pillow several times and in several different ways before eventually settling down. I was reminded of the way a dog will sometimes circle and paw at an area before lying down, but I wisely kept that thought to myself. She did catch us watching her and sarcastically asked if didn't we have something else to do. We wisely remained silent and made a show of pretending to be busy until it was apparent that she was settled and ready for Clem to begin his story.

7

Clem poured himself a glass of water. It was so quiet that the silence was a 4th presence in the room that none of us acknowledged, even though all of us were aware of it. Even though the drapes were closed, I knew by the change that had come over the room that the sun had set and that it was dark outside. This stillness only made the surroundings in this room seem more surreal, but in a comfortable and familiar way. I could not shake the feeling that we were now disconnected from present, and had I not known better, I would have sworn we had gone many decades back in time. The style of the furniture, the overall décor of the room, the types of lamps in use, the pendulum clocks and the old portraits on the wall, the hides on the floor, and the guns on the fireplace; all of these things combined to give a feeling of detachment from modern living. Only the kitchen with its relatively modern appliances, and the other rooms with their electric lights, reminded me that we were still in the present.

This family room even smelled old, but not in a bad way. It was one of the first things I noticed when Daisy and I stepped over the threshold. It reminded me of the office my father worked in when I was a boy. My father and grandfather were attorneys and they shared an office in the small southern town I grew up in. The office at one time was a separate building which served as the cook room in the house my father grew up in. It was moved and converted into an office when the house was renovated back in the late 50's. The office kept the original wooden floors and paneled walls. However, it was upgraded with air conditioning window units and indoor plumbing. As a child, I was sometimes allowed to come into the office on those especially hot and humid southern summer days. The temperature inside felt as if it were just a degree or two above freezing, and it felt delicious after being out in the sweltering heat. I would be directed to sit in one of the uncomfortable wooden chairs that were reserved for clients, but during the times I was allowed in the office, there were no clients present. Even when the only people in the office were my father, my grandfather, and the secretary they shared, I was still told to sit still and remain quiet. The furnishings consisted of a couple of old desks and some barrister bookcases similar to the ones in Clem's family room. The desks were made of wood and were filled with cubby holes and drawers. Sometimes, the legal secretary would feel sorry for me and invite me to sit by her and have a cold bottle of coke and some salted peanuts while she did some typing or filing. I still remember the way that office smelled, and I can still recall that the smell could be especially strong when a desk drawer was opened. It was an old smell; musty, a little heavy, bookish, and smelled as if it were full of memories. That is what the smell in Clem's sitting room reminded me of.

But there was more in Clem's family room that really added to this feeling of being detached from modern living. There was no TV, no radio, no computer, and no electronic device of any type to interrupt and demand our attention. The only sounds were slow methodical and almost hypnotic sounds of the clocks ticking, and the sounds we made as we settled into our chairs and couch and sipped our beverages and nibbled our snacks. Even though it had been quite warm during the day, the house in general, and this room in particular, maintained a very pleasant temperature. This air conditioned climate control was the one obvious modern day luxury that was welcome.

Clem was now ready to begin his story and he assumed the attitude of a school teacher about to impart his vast knowledge to a couple of ignorant and wayward pupils. "You may not remember," Clem began, "but the western frontier was looked upon as a land of adventure and romance, not only by the people who lived in America, but also by people who lived in Europe, especially England. You also may not realize that the educated classes in Britain had been reading stories of the American West and following your migration with excited interest. The British fascination with the Indians, with the bountiful and exotic game for hunting, and with the wild and unbound vastness of the American west was due in part to the stories of James Fennimore Cooper and in part to stories told by previous English travelers who had come to the American West, and returned to England with their tales and trophies. And, just to add a bit more fuel, the publishing of the journal of Lewis and Clark added to this fascination."

"So, in 1846, my great-great grandfather made up his mind that he had to experience this for himself. He kept a journal, a very few pages of which still survive and are in these bookcases you see in this room. He also passed down stories orally to his sons. Some of his sons accompanied him back to America on another trip several years later. These sons kept their own journals and added these oral stories that their father had told them to their own writings. So, the story I am about to tell you came from these written and oral stories that have been passed down through the generations."

"My great-great-grandfather's name was Roland and I will refer to him by that name for the rest of the story. So, like I said, Roland came to America in 1846 and he brought with him a couple of his favorite servants, his hunting dogs, and his sporting guns. It was not common, but it was also not unheard of for wealthy Europeans to come to America and travel in such a way; and while Roland was not the first Englishman the Americans had seen travelling this way, the sight of a man travelling in such a way still stood out and attracted onlookers. In later years, after the west opened up more and the trails became better and safer, some Europeans would travel not only with their servants and their dogs, but they also outfitted their own wagon trains in order to carry their furniture, their favorite food and beverages, and even their bathtubs. These rich adventurers wanted to see and experience the west; they just did not want to be uncomfortable while doing so."

"At that time, the untamed American West had as its starting point the western boundary of the state of Missouri. Missouri had only become a state 25 years before, in 1821, and the state itself was pretty much still unsettled. The land to the west of Missouri's western boundary had not been fully explored, much less fully mapped, and there were great swaths of land that were marked "Unknown" or simply "Indian Territory" on the maps of the day. However, on the eastern edge of the state, the city of St. Louis on the Mississippi River was bustling. It was both a destination for some and a starting point for those who wished to continue on and travel further north or west. From St. Louis, a traveler could obtain all the goods and provisions needed to begin such an adventure, and if the traveler did not already have a guide, then there were plenty of men in the city who were willing to hire themselves out as guides."

"River boats of all types would sometimes be lined up along the shore, waiting for a spot at Laclede's Landing to load and unload their passengers and sometimes their cargo. Once provisioned, the traveler could take a steamboat north up the Mississippi river for about 10 miles to the confluence of Missouri River and the Mississippi River. At this river junction, the traveler had several options to choose from. He could stay on the Mississippi River and travel north, moving along the boundary of Missouri and Illinois. If he chose to continue further north, then he could remain on the same river and steam along the boundary of Iowa and Illinois. Assuming he continued along far enough, he would eventually reach the boundary of northern Indian Territory. This area would become the state of Michigan later that year and then the state of Minnesota ten years later."

"Or if he did not want to take the Mississippi River north, then he could follow the Missouri River west from this same junction and cross the state of Missouri until he reached the very edge of the eastern section of Indian Territory. From here, he could choose from two overland jumping off points. The traveler could choose the Oregon Trail and head northwest or the traveler could take the Santé Fe Trail and head southwest.

Of course, there was always the option to simply stay on the Missouri river and travel north and then west as far as the boat would go, hugging the western boundary of Iowa and then entering the portion of Indian Territory that would become the state of Nebraska within the next 20 years. From there it was possible to travel further into Indian Territory, into an area that would become the states of South Dakota, North Dakota, and Montana in about 40 years. Either choice was sure to lead to adventure, sport, hunting, and manly competition. In short, everything a man of means needed in order to participate in a test of self, which was important to men of that time period in England."

"Roland stayed in America, on this initial trip, for about 2 years. During this time, he saw Indians in their natural element, hunted with Mountain Men, and mingled with trappers. He followed rivers from their source all the way to their mouth and rafted down rapids that ran through canyons. He drank with both Negroes and white men. He drank with rough men; some of whom were running from their past, some who were dreaming of a better future, and some who were wanted by the law. One thing all of these white and black men had in common was the hope that the West would provide an opportunity for a new life, where the only thing that mattered was the present and the future, not the past. Few people cared who your father was. None of them cared that the land they were entering and claiming had been home to Indians for generations. The fact that none of these men cared what the Indians hoped for was another thing these men had in common."

"These people that Roland came into contact with were a diverse group and unlike any men he had ever come into contact with before. He always said that he was impartial in his prejudices, which was really not true, but was apparently one thing that Roland liked to often say. When not getting to know his fellow man better, he spent his time chasing Buffalo from horseback, and experiencing many other harrowing adventures on the plains and rivers. However, his main goal was to shoot every beast and form of game that appeared; particularly

Grizzly bear and Buffalo. He said that there was something unique about the American West that was difficult to explain and it had to be experienced in order to understand. It was as if the very air was purer than any air he had ever breathed, and that the sky was larger than any sky he had ever seen, and the stars were more brilliant than any stars he had ever looked upon. Even the moon looked bigger and seemed to hang lower in the sky than it did anywhere else. He said that when standing in that vast openness he had felt more alive, more alone, and yet more in touch with the earth than at any other time in his life. He compared the prairie to a landlocked waterless ocean that stretched before you, unchanging to the horizon; and once this prairie had been entered, it was not long before you found yourself surrounded by it to the extent that nothing else could be seen, no matter which direction you turned. It was a sight that he could not have imagined and would not have believed existed, had he not seen it himself."

"The family story goes that he would get a faraway look in his eye when he was talking about the West. Then he would get quiet and say, 'The water, let me tell you about the water,' as if he were talking about the Holy Grail. He said that water was a key element in the West because of its scarcity, and because of this scarcity, he believed that the people in the West thought about water in a completely different way than people in the eastern part of America and in England did. The water in the mountain streams was so clean and clear that he said you could actually stand on the bank, look at the water, and not only count the pebbles on the bottom but tell their color. If it were the right time of morning, and if the sun could be caught at the right angle so that it was shining into instead of reflecting off of the water, then the color of the pebbles would be so vivid that it would seem like you were looking at something so beautiful and perfect that it was hard to believe it was naturally occurring and not something that had been preserved under glass in a museum. He sometimes referred to the sight in shallow water as watching miniature rapids made by small rocky ripples. This water was so clear that the depth was sometimes deceiving. He said that on more than one occasion he would step into a stream that he thought was only knee-to-waist deep, only to find himself in water that was several feet over his head. He finally learned to not entirely trust what his eyes were telling him."

"At the end of his almost two year adventure, he returned to St. Louis a wiser and more experienced man. It was now early 1848, and the first thing he did was to hire a local man and charge him with the duties of making the preparations and the purchases necessary for his return trip. He hoped to return in about a year, sometime in late 1849 or early 1850. Of course, the man he chose was recommended by his new found friends and was known to be completely reliable. Roland had learned to be overly cautious, and just to make sure of this man's reliability, my great-great grandfather paid him exceedingly well. This, he believed, would ensure the man's complete devotion to him. However, as I said, Roland was a cautious man. To make doubly sure of the man's devotion, Roland left one of his most trusted servants, Ethan, behind on the pretense of assisting the newly hired man. The intent was to not only be of assistance but to mainly keep his eyes and ears open for any business or adventure opportunities that may arise, and then to communicate that intelligence back to Roland in England as soon as possible. Roland was now confident, that when he returned to America, he would know that everything would be ready and he would not have to personally go about getting provisions and a guide like he had on this trip. He hoped in the meantime to profit financially from his choice to leave Ethan behind, who was tasked with the responsibility of finding business opportunities. At this point, he decided to return to England. He had stories and trophies of his own to share and tell about, and he had the knowledge that he had people on the ground in America working for him, who had his interests at heart."

"Upon arriving back home, he knew he needed to convince his youngest sons to return to America with him. He would leave his oldest son behind to oversee the family property and collect the rents and other income. It was the British tradition at the time that the oldest son would inherit all lands and tenants and property. So, it made sense that the oldest should stay in Britain and oversee all of it. It was the 3 youngest sons who would not inherit any property. Don't misunderstand; they would be well off financially, they just would not have anything to do other than spend whatever money he left to them. He faced the same dilemma with his younger sons that all fathers of his class faced at the time, and that was what to do with the youngest sons. These 4 sons were his only children."

At this point in the story, I motioned to Clem, got his attention, and pointed at Daisy. She had fallen asleep on the couch. I had been watching her struggle to stay awake for the last half an hour and she finally gave up just a couple of minutes ago. Of course, she was too hardheaded to just ask Clem to stop so she could go to bed. It was just like her to not admit defeat but to try and fight through the exhaustion in hopes that one of us would give in before she did. I looked at my watch and saw that it was only 9:45 but it sure felt later.

Clem stopped talking and looked at her and then smiled. He stretched his arms over his head, yawned and said, "Yes, it is getting late and the two of you have had a very long day. We can talk some more tomorrow after the two of you have had a good night of rest."

I thanked him and then tried to stand. My knee had gotten stiff in the time that I had been sitting and it was with a little difficulty that I was able to get out of the chair and stand. Clem laughed at me and mentioned that he seemed to be able to get around better on one leg than I could on two at the present time.

I hobbled over to the couch where she was sleeping and tried to wake her. I could not get her to stir, it was only by repeatedly calling her name and gently shaking her shoulder she finally responded and mumbled, "Just leave me here to sleep." I was really tired myself and too tired to try and convince her to get up and come to bed. So, I just left her there on the couch to spend the night.

Before heading to bed, I cleared away the dishes and cups and trays and took them back to the kitchen. Clem followed me with the coffee pot which he sat in the sink. "I don't usually lock the doors at night because it is just me here and there has never been any real reason to lock the doors, but since you all are here, I will lock the back door just to be safe. The front door has a deadbolt lock on it, please lock it when you go back that way," he said to me. He then locked the back door and disappeared into his bedroom only to return a few minutes later with a patchwork quilt that looked to have been made by hand many years ago.

He looked at me and said, "Lay this over her. She may get chilly during the night. My wife made it years ago and it really is quite soft and warm. Also, please turn out the oil and gas lamps in the family room, but leave the electric light on in the bathroom as she probably will not know where she is if she wakes up during the night and there is no point in distressing her. Just leave these dishes and we can wash them in the morning."

I took the comforter and thanked him as he headed back to his bedroom. He called out "good night" as he closed the door that led to his room.

I hobbled back into the family room and tried once more to wake her up. Failing in that, I covered her with the quilt, picked up my gun and gun belt, locked the deadbolt, and headed down the hallway to our rooms. I stopped in the bathroom and turned the light on and left the door open as Clem had requested. It provided plenty of light if either of us woke up during the night. At the first bedroom, I looked in and saw her clothes were laid out on the bed but I did not see mine. I continued down to the second bedroom where I found my clothes laid out on that bed. I got the hint and was too beat to think about why she had separated us like that. I closed the door, turned the light out, undressed in the dark, and crawled into bed. I remember thinking how peaceful and quiet everything was. All I could hear was the clocks ticking in the family room and a pack of coyotes howling somewhere in the distant night. The light from the hall bathroom reflected under the bedroom door and it reminded me of something that I could not quite put my finger on. It was only a matter of minutes before I was sound asleep too.

8

The sun rises early in Arizona during the summer months and on that particular June morning it rose at 5:14. If that is not early enough, the sky starts to get light about a half hour prior to actual sun rise. I know the time of the sunrise that day, because in my haste to get into bed, I had forgotten to pull the shades completely closed in the bedroom. There was a crack between them just big enough to let in just enough light to wake me. For a few moments, I was confused as to where I was. I swung my legs out over the double bed and held my head in my hands. Slowly, the fog of sleep lifted and the memory of yesterday and where we were came flooding back. My knee was throbbing but felt a little better. My stings were also feeling better. I looked at my watch, registered the time, limped out of bed, and jerked the shades fully closed. The house was just as still and quiet as it was the night before. I limped back to bed and fell immediately back to sleep.

I slept another two hours and would have slept even longer had I not been awakened by the sound of voices and the smell of coffee. I quickly dressed into my clean jeans and shirt and headed down the hallway towards her room. The door was open and the bed had been slept in, so I knew that sometime during the night she had gotten up and found her way to her bedroom. Turning the corner to the family room, I was greeted by Clem with a rousing "Good morning, Doc! How is the knee today?" He motioned me over to have a seat as he proceeded to pour me a cup of coffee, black with no sweetener.

"Morning, Clem," I said. "It is still stiff and sore but coming along. Something sure smells good."

He noticed me looking around and said, "Daisy insisted on making breakfast this morning, so she is in the kitchen whipping up some pancakes and sausage." I looked at him to see if he was kidding. He did not appear to be, so I nodded and took a sip of the coffee. "She was not too happy with us for leaving her on the couch last night; but once I explained to her how she had refused to move, and how we tried to help her to bed, and how she told us to leave her there, she then soon understood and got over it and came around."

"Good coffee, thanks Clem." Then I asked, "How long have you been up?"

"Just long enough to wash the dishes from last night, make a pot of coffee, and show Daisy where the fixings were for pancakes. She was up just a little before me. She was looking at the stuff in the bookcases when I came in."

"Yes, I'd like to take a closer look at your things too while you explain them to us. Daisy and I really love history and artifacts and the tales behind them, and it sure looks like you have a very well preserved collection here. Are they all family related?"

"Pretty much everything is family related," he said. "The things that you see here were either directly owned by ancestors or are here to confirm a story about an ancestor. Anyway, I would love to go through these things with the two of you. We still need to finish where I left off last night, but we have time to do both. I was talking to Daisy earlier this morning about how long you can stay here. She said that you both are on a vacation and really have no plans for the next day or two, so I was hoping you would consider spending some extra time here with me."

I did not respond but he apparently saw the shadow of doubt cross my face because he continued, "I know it may be a lot to ask. I am old and a stranger to you both, but I really enjoy the company. There are a few chores you can help me with, so you don't have to feel like a free-loader. Don't be cross with me, but I mentioned this to Daisy already this morning. She said that it would be fine with her but that I would need to talk to you as the choice is yours."

"It does not surprise me that she would say that. Let me think about it, Clem. It is true that we are on a vacation of sorts and really have no plans for the next couple of days. I have not spoken to Daisy yet, but I am sure she enjoyed your story as much as I did last night and is looking forward to hearing more of it. Plus, I am intrigued by your collection here as much as she is." I paused for a moment and stroked my chin and then continued, "If Daisy said it was ok with her if we stay a day or two longer, then I have no objection. There is one condition, however, and that is that you will let us help you with whatever chores you want to have done. If that is agreeable to you then we will stay for another day or two.

He broke out into a big grin and said, "Fair enough Doc."

As if on cue, Daisy popped her head around the corner and with a big smile on her face announced that breakfast was ready.

"Morning, Doc?" she said looking directly at me. Which was followed by "Good lord, it sure did not take you long to get Clem to start calling you that." "You see, Clem," she still had her eyes on me and continued, "He has this wish to live in the old west and die in a gun fight on some dusty deserted street."

"Only partly true," I corrected. "Yes, I wish I did live in the old west. That part is true and it is also true that I would like to have been in a gun fight. However, I do not want to die in a gunfight; I would have just liked to have been in one. There is a slight but significant difference there." Then I changed the subject and asked, "Why the big smile? I know you and kitchens mix as well as oil and water."

"I still hate working in a kitchen, but I was eavesdropping and I heard you say we could stay a couple more days and that is why I am smiling."

I was pretty sure that I had said we would stay an extra day or two. I don't think I said that we would stay an extra couple of more days, but I was hungry and did not feel like starting an argument that I would most likely lose. Besides, it really did not matter to me if we stayed an extra day or if we stayed the entire week. I was ok with either as long as she was happy and we were back and ready for work on time.

After breakfast, Clem offered to show us around outside. I was struck again, just as I had been when Daisy and I first parked in the front driveway, by how quiet it was. There were no birds singing or even flying today, there were no dogs barking, there was just no sound at all other than the sounds the three of us made and the gentle rustling of the slight breeze as it disturbed the dead palm fronds around us. Clem led us out the back door and it was apparent that as nice as the house was on the front porch and on the inside, the back was a stark contrast. The only way to describe it is to call it a mess. I was reminded of a movie I saw a few years ago about these people who went to this isolated bar. The bar was in pretty good shape when viewed from the front and from the inside, but when the camera panned around to the back of the bar, it consisted of centuries old ruins and portrayed decay and neglect. Of course, the bar was home to vampires too. While Clem's backyard was not centuries old and there were not any vampires, the level of decay and neglect were the same. The roof was in serious need of repair. The porch was indeed a wrap-around porch, as I had originally thought, but the railings had fallen down on the back and far side of the house, and most of the porch floor boards were missing. The yard was a complete disaster. I already explained how the front yard looked and the backyard was even worse. The weeds were waist high. The palm trees that lined the front driveway did continue all the way around the backyard, and then beyond the line of palm trees was an overgrown wildness of what was part of the same field that we drove through in the front. If it had not been for the trees marking the boundary between yard and field, then there would have been no way to tell the difference. That is how bad it was. Clem walked us over to the back left corner of the yard and pointed out the huge cement hole that was once a very nice swimming pool. It had steep curving sides and the deep end looked to be 9 or 10 feet deep. There was a built in hot tub off the shallow end of the pool. The cement was cracked and the pool was full of debris and trash.

The bottom also may have served as the final resting place for the skeletal remains of any animals that had fallen or strayed into the deep end and then were unable to get out. It was beyond salvaging, if anyone had any ideas about ever using it again. The best thing to do would be to fill it in and plant flowers over it.

We continued around the perimeter as Clem continued his tour. There were several outbuildings and an open sided covered garage where Clem's truck and my jeep were parked. The outbuildings looked as if they had not been used in years. One had completely collapsed upon itself and the other four looked to be waiting for a similar fate. Clem explained that these buildings had been storage sheds and workshops when the place was a working farm, but that they had been emptied of their contents long ago and were now just shells. He pointed to a line of low hills off in the distance and explained that the base of those hills marked the end of the field about 1 and three quarters of a mile away. Although not visible from here, he told us that along the line where the field met the base of the hill were concrete foundations and brick chimneys. These ruins are all that remain of what used to be living quarters for the migrant workers who would come up from Mexico each season to help with the harvest. He then went on for some time explaining how the migrant workers lived and travelled as a group, some of these groups included several generations of the same family.

Clem was looking off towards the low hills as he explained, "Usually, the same groups of Mexican relatives and families would come up every season to work the same farms, and it was like a big reunion each year. They would arrive throughout the day in a caravan of old assorted vehicles, and that evening I would throw a big cook out to kick off the season. My wife and the women would set the tables and slice and prepare the fruit and vegetables. The men would cook hamburgers, chicken, and ribs over a huge open fire grill. My boys and the workers' kids would play games and swim in the pool. Then, the next morning, the men would all meet me at sunrise and we would walk the fields together. We would assign work teams and duties that included everyone, determine where we would start, and then we would establish and agree upon daily quotas so that we could measure our progress. After we had our plan, everyone would break off into groups and finish getting settled into their quarters, and prepare for work to start early the following morning. It was all very well organized and everyone worked very hard, but we had some fun moments as well."

He then looked up at me and said, "You never told me what you do for a living Doc."

"Well, Clem, I used to be a gynecologist," I said. "But I had to give it up."

"Oh, why was that?" he asked.

"I kept getting in trouble for bringing my work home with me," was my deadpan reply.

Clem doubled up in laughter. He was laughing so hard that I thought he would lose a lung and fall off of his crutch.

"Jeez, Doc," Daisy said rolling her eyes. "You are so full of shit that it amazes me that your eyes are blue and not brown." She was smiling when she said this.

Turning my gaze back to Clem, "I am an actuary for an insurance company," I said.

"I see, so you are pretty good at risk management. Correct?" Clem asked.

Before I could respond, Daisy chimed in. "Yes, Clem that is it in a nutshell. Doc's work requires that he be both analytical and that he understand human behavior, and with those skills he attempts to assess risk and then determine the probability of certain events occurring and the contingent outcomes of those events. It is all very mathematical and logical with some hocus pocus mixed in as well."

"I guess that is the job description," I said. "However, I prefer to think of it differently. My approach is that life is a series of choices and every outcome is the result of some previous choice. Understand the choices that are made, and the reasons and circumstances underlying the choice, and then you can determine if a pattern exists, which thus enables you to anticipate the probable consequences."

I could hear her sigh and mumble something that sounded like, "here we go again."

So, I changed tack and dropped the discussion of choices and continued, "But, getting back to why we are out here, we agreed that we would help you with some chores. It is obvious that a lot needs to be done out here, and I was wondering where you would like us to start and what would you like us to do?"

"Oh, nothing back here," he replied. "It would take 40 men with a truck a month of Sundays to do what needs to be done back here." He looked around and dropped his hand to his side as if the thought of all that needed to be done was more weight than he could bear. The he continued, "To be honest, I don't think it is worth the effort. Too much time has passed where it has been neglected; but I remember our agreement and I would like you and Daisy to help me clean up the family burial plot, particularly around my wife's grave."

He then pointed out into the field and my gaze followed his outstretched arm to a clump of bushes and trees about a hundred yards away. I had not noticed it earlier; it blended in and was just another part of the overall overgrowth that surrounded us. As I looked closer, I could see that there was a clump of broken trees and bushes that were enclosed by what looked like a small wrought iron fence. I squinted, trying to force my eyes to a sharper focus until I could see that within the enclosure, there was something white reflecting in the sun.

Clem led the way, using his crutch both to walk and to test the ground in front for rattle snakes and hopefully scatter any he found. We followed single file just behind him, with Daisy bringing up the rear. The gate through the iron fence had fallen off its hinges and was lying off to the side. The rest of the fence was still standing and it was overall in pretty good shape, it just needed some repair in spots and some shoring up. It reminded me of the fence I had come across with my friend Sandy, when we were out looking for the old town in the desert that I mentioned earlier. In fact, this fence was so similar to that one that it could have been the same fence, only 140 years later. I guess cemetery fence technology does not need to change all that much. We stood there in silence as our eyes took in this tiny family cemetery. The openness of the field in which we were in, and the smallness of this cemetery, made me feel small and quiet inside. It was a very small plot in terms of area, and there was just enough room for the three of us to stand inside the broken fence, which completely surrounded the burial area. The plot was overgrown with weeds and briar bushes and other dead vegetation; it was so overgrown that the ground was covered and could not be seen, but it did indeed have two white marble tombstones. One was carved with only Clem's name and date of birth. The other was carved:

Anne Powell
Loving Wife and Mother
Born February 9, 1934
Died April 27, 1992

According to those dates, she had been dead for 21 years and was 58 years old when she died.

After a few minutes, I broke the silence by turning towards Clem and asking, "There appears to be something missing from her headstone, Clem. I don't see the usual 'Gone But Not Forgotten' phrase. Did you forget to add it?"

Clem responded, "Nope, I did not forget to add it. I intentionally did not add it. I figured that Anne will be forgotten once I die. I am pretty sure that I am the only one that remembers her. I am the only living person who can recall the way her hair smelled after she washed it, or how contagious her laugh could be, or how pretty she was on our wedding day, or how soft and kind her eyes were. I don't think anyone else is around to remember those things. Anne put up with a lot from me when she was living; I did not want to add something that I knew was misleading and hypocritical once she was dead. Just like many others who came before her, now that she is gone she will soon be forgotten. I am pretty sure the same will apply to me once I am gone. "

I smiled and said, "Believe it or not Clem, I understand and completely agree with your reasoning and your explanation." Then, looking over at the other grave, I continued "So, that is where your other leg is, huh? I asked as I pointed to the grave that had his tombstone over it.

"Yep. It will hold the rest of me one day too, I suppose."

"We would be happy to clear this plot up for you Clem and make some repairs to the fence as well. I am sure we can make it very pretty again fairly quickly."

Clem looked at me and smiled. He did not speak and he did not have to speak; I could see in his eyes how grateful he was.

After a few more minutes, I asked the question that had been on my mind all day "What happened here, Clem?"

"What do you mean?" he responded.

"Well, it is obvious that this was once a very large and prosperous farm operation, and from what you have told me, it appears that you and your family lived a very comfortable lifestyle. However, now that is all gone and it appears to have been gone for a long time. I am just curious what happened, if you don't mind me asking."

"I don't mind you asking at all, Doc. Part of the story of what happened here lies in the history I was telling you about my ancestors last night, and I will continue that story later today. Then, you will understand the way I came to own this land and live here with my family and farm it successfully for so many years. That will be a long but easy story to tell. The hard part is telling you how all of that success came to the neglected ruins that you see here now."

Sensing that we may have been exceeding our bounds, Daisy contributed, "You don't have to go into any more detail than you are comfortable with, Clem. You don't owe us any explanations and if we cross any lines with our curiosity, then please know. It is unintentional and all you have to do is tell us to back off."

"You are sweet, but it is fine, Daisy. It was my idea to tell you this story and it is natural that you will have questions along the way. So, don't worry honey. I don't think there are any lines that are too personal for you to cross, but if we come upon one, then I will let you know," was Clem's response. "Now, how about we head back to the house? I can fix some sandwiches and then, after we eat, if you are both up for it, we can come back out here and tackle this clean up. I have a few yard implements and other tools in the back of my pickup."

As we turned to go back towards the house, Clem took the lead again. We had only taken a few steps when I asked about his boys. "You mentioned your sons would play with the worker's kids and we have seen their bedrooms. I was curious, where your boys are now, Clem?"

He stopped but did not turn around. Instead, he just stood there, supporting himself with his crutch and looking towards the house. The breeze moved through the brush around us and made a loud rattling sound, which we all mistook at first for a snake. Then, he began to speak. "Wesley, my oldest son, was a bit of a loner and a rambler and was never one to stay put here. I truly believe that some people have a tortured soul. I am not sure if this is something they are born with, or if it is something that is shaped by the events in their life. Whichever it is, Wesley was one of those people. He did not socialize a great deal, but the people he was drawn to the most, and who were also drawn to him, were also tortured souls or at least troubled. He dropped out of high school in his junior year and went to Texas where he drifted for a while. He eventually ended up working on oil rigs. He did that for many years, working on rigs in Texas and the Gulf of Mexico. He would come home about once a year to visit and then would be off again. One day, I received a letter from him, just a few days before his 31st birthday, saying he was quitting the oil work and was going with a group of men he had met up to Alaska. They were going to do some gold prospecting in the interior and that he would write me another letter once he got settled. That was in 1987 and it was the last I ever heard from him. We filed a missing persons report and some detectives came out to talk to me and my wife, but they had no leads and the investigation never even really got off the ground. He left Texas, but never reached Alaska. He was born a free spirit and he died a free spirit; he just simply disappeared from the face of the earth."

"John, my youngest son, was the ambitious one. He finished high school and then graduated from ASU with a degree in Architecture. While he was attending college, he met a girl from Oklahoma and they were married a year after graduation. They lived in Phoenix and would come home to visit about once a month and spend the weekend with us while Anne was alive. After Anne died, their visits became less frequent and they would rarely spend the weekend; I would see them once every other month or so. They both seemed very happy but were never able to have children. I think they would have stayed in Arizona and made a life here, but after living here for several years, his wife began to miss Oklahoma and wanted to be closer to her family. So, they moved back to a small town near Oklahoma City where John was able to find an even better job. They were both killed in a tornado in 1994. He was 32 years old. There were only a few remains that were found of both of them, and those few remains are buried in a single casket in Oklahoma."

When he finished speaking, Clem wiped the sleeve of his shirt across his face and then struck the ground with the end of his crutch and spit off into the brush. Then he started walking back towards the house. His pace was a little slower than before.

No one spoke for the rest of the walk back.

But once we arrived back at the house, Clem was his usual cheery self again. He went right to work fixing some sandwiches, as promised, and Daisy assisted to keep him company, of course. While they were doing that, I went out to his pickup truck to see what type of tools he had. I found an ax, a swing blade, a shovel, a pair of hedge trimmers, and an assortment of screwdrivers, pliers, hammers, nails, screws, and a spool of wire. Not much, but all we needed to clean up the cemetery, I thought. Daisy joined me as I started to unload these tools from his truck to tell me that lunch was ready. After looking over our inventory of tools, we walked back inside the house together.

Right after lunch, the three of us trudged back out to the cemetery, each of us carrying tools. I used the ax to cut down some of the larger unwanted bushes and then used the swing blade to clear the weeds. It was easy to dispose of the cuttings; I just dragged them about 20 feet outside of the fence area and dropped them there. Daisy worked with Clem to re-hang the gate using the wire and some screws, and when they had completed that, the three of us worked together to make some repairs to the fence. Between Clem hobbling around on one leg, me still puffy from the bee stings and limping with my sore knee, Daisy also still puffy from bee stings and with a red scar on her cheek, I imagine we would have provided comic relief if anyone had observed us. We did not talk much other than small talk, mingled with a series of questions and instructions that came up as we performed our tasks. It took us about 4 hours to finish and it was almost 5 o'clock when the last piece of fence was braced and we were done.

We all stood back to admire our work and it really did look nice. Daisy was standing between us, and put her arms around each of us as we complemented each other on a job well done. We were all sweating and a bit tired.

"It sure looks nice," said Clem. "I cannot thank either of you enough. I should have never allowed it to get this out of control, but then once it had, there was nothing I could do by myself to clean it up."

"Oh, be quiet, Clem," Daisy said. "We are happy to have helped you do this and are still happy to help you with anything else you want done. There is one thing that I think is missing though."

Without another word, she turned and ran back towards the house. She returned a few minutes later with her yellow sun dress and a pair of scissors. "I had this in the jeep," she said as she held up her dress for Clem to see. "I think your wife's grave could use a little color." And she walked through the gate and began to cut the dress into strips of yellow fabric. She used one of the shorter strips to tie her hair back. She then tied the longer strips together to make one long piece of yellow fabric which she then used to tie a bow around Anne's tombstone.

She then rejoined us outside the fence.

"That looks very nice, honey. Anne would like that," Clem said as he hugged her.

"Yes, it does look very nice, Daisy. It was sweet of you to do that," I said. That is what I said, but what I was thinking was that it sure was a shame to do that because she sure did look good in that sun dress, especially when that dress and a straw hat were all she was wearing.

We were just getting ready to pick up our tools and head back when Clem added, "Well, there is one more thing you can do for me." Before we could ask what, he continued "I took a chicken out to thaw and it should be ready for the oven by now. While I get that started, Daisy would you mind doing another load of wash? I know you two are limited in what you have to wear and you both are quite dirty and smelly after today's work." Then, looking at me, he had to add, "Especially you, Doc. Then, once you get the clothes started, I could sure use some help cutting up some vegetables. Then, you and I can go get cleaned up while Doc monitors the cooking and moves the clothes to the dryer. After we have cleaned up and eaten, then we will make some coffee and I will pick up where we left off last night and we can talk until we are ready for bed, or until Daisy falls asleep on the couch again."

And with that, we headed back to the house for the second time that day. Clem went in to get supper working, and I went down to the shower, while Daisy started the laundry and then went to help Clem with the vegetables. It was starting to feel more like we were family, instead of strangers who were guests.

The laundry finished while Clem was in his room cleaning up, and I could hear him shuffling about, while Daisy was also cleaning up down the hallway in the bathroom we shared. When the dryer finished, I removed her clothes and my clothes, folded them, and then headed down the hall way towards our bedrooms, carrying the clean clothes in my arms. I paused by the bathroom door just as the water in the shower stopped running. I tried to open the door but it was locked. I knocked and said that I had her clean clothes, and if she would open the door, then I would set them on the vanity. Her reply was that she still needed to condition her hair and for me to just set her clothes on the floor in the hallway just outside the door. It was obvious that she did not want me to come into the bathroom and run the risk of me joining her in the shower. So, I did exactly as she asked me to do and placed her clothes on the floor just outside the door. I laid the piece of yellow ribbon on top of the pile of clothes in case she wanted to tie her back with it again. Then, I walked down to what I now considered to be my own room and changed back into my clean jeans and shirt and boots. I left the gun and gun belt in the room, hanging from a peg on the wall that I assumed was meant to be a place from which to hang a hat.

9

After an excellent dinner, we basically repeated the routine of the night before. Each of us pitched in to wash and put away the dishes. Then coffee was made and we each brought coffee and cakes and trays and cups from the kitchen to the family room. It was just after 7:30, and although the sun would not set for about another 15 minutes, Clem went around the room and lit the lamps on the tables and the one central ceiling light. Once again, I had the impression of how just that one simple act had the effect of turning the calendar back 100 years. The clocks on the walls and mantel were ticking and those were once again the only other sounds except those made by us as we settled in. I made a mental note to buy some oil lamps and candles and clocks for my house when this trip was over, and to convert my den into a room resembling this one. Clem and I once again choose the red leather chairs while Daisy once again made herself a nest of pillows on the couch.

Clem began, "It was early spring 1852, before Roland could return to America. He had wanted to return within a year of his last trip but circumstances at home caused him to delay this return trip. As a result, over 5 years had passed since the beginning of his first trip to America, and over 3 years had passed since he had left America and returned to England. However, there were also circumstances occurring in America that worked to his advantage. Had he not chosen to delay his return trip, then it is possible he may have missed out on one of the most profitable time periods in his life. One of the fortunate things that had happened during this time was that Ethan, the servant he had left behind in St. Louis, had been providing him with excellent business news, which Roland was able to take advantage of. One of these news events, was the 1848-49 discovery of gold in California. As a result of this, there was a virtual stampede of men wanting to take their chance at striking it rich. These men added to the already growing numbers of people heading west through St. Louis. All of these people needed to be outfitted and provisioned for the trip west, and Roland's servant, Ethan, in St. Louis saw a money making opportunity. He established himself as a middle man between the merchants who sold the provisions and the guides who led the westward bound fortune seekers. The fact that he had himself already made a two year excursion west gave him immediate credibility with all parties. He made an arrangement with both merchants and guides and he was able to negotiate discounted rates for provisions, tools, animals, and everything else these prospectors and travelers needed. As a result, the guides would come to him with their orders, he would then go to the merchants and purchase the goods, then mark them up for resale back to the guides. Even with the markup, his prices were lower than the guides could get on their own. He made a handsome profit, which he then passed along to Roland. Roland saw the advantage of this arrangement and began to fund other business opportunities that Ethan brought to his attention."

"From this humble beginning as a middle man between merchants and travelers, Roland was able to invest the profits and began to accumulate and invest in an assortment of opportunities: land along proposed westward land routes and along the banks of the largest rivers, including the Mississippi, the Ohio, and the Missouri; cattle; warehouses; and even a couple of steamboats. The railroads were in their infancy and most of the ones in America at this time were located in the Eastern States; mainly Maryland, Pennsylvania, New Jersey, and New York. However, there was one little known twist that the servant took full advantage of. That twist was, that also in 1849, the Pacific Railroad was chartered in St. Louis with the mission to connect St. Louis to the western boundary of the State and eventually extend the rail line all the way to the

Pacific Ocean. Due to delays, groundbreaking did not occur for another two years, and the railroad did not receive its first steam powered locomotive until mid-1852, when it arrived by steamboat. The engine held its inaugural run in December of that year, making a run of only a few minutes to an outlying St. Louis neighborhood. That was a minor accomplishment; it was the future expansion of railroads and the promise the railroads held as a way to move both people, goods, and mail that was recognized by Roland's servant. So, he did some speculative investing in this new form of transportation, which paid off in multiplies of more than 100 times the original investment. Ethan was handsomely rewarded for his good sense and his honesty. As a result, this humble servant was able to purchase a large tract of land for himself and build a fine house high on a hill overlooking the river outside of St. Louis. He retired comfortably soon after Roland returned to St. Louis, and although he no longer needed to travel or work for my ancestor, he remained a loyal and true friend to Roland and his sons. He never married, and died in 1866. He left his property and fortune to charity."

Clem paused here and said, "I am getting ahead of myself, but you two are smart enough to figure out that these investments are the basis for the wealth that the descendants of Roland, myself included, benefited from. He continued to accumulate land and property rights and businesses in America. Some of these land holdings were sold to speculators back in England, who had the idea of building English-like towns on the prairie. I know that this may sound odd to you, but there was quite a bit of interest in establishing these English towns in the 1870s and 1880s. These towns had mixed success, but my ancestors did not really care how the towns fared, as they had already made their money when they sold the land to the speculators. Some of the other land holdings were sold to the railroads, some was sold to settlers who followed, some of the land was kept and leased out, and some of the land was traded for land further west. So in effect, my ancestors, who were already rich, continued to get even richer.

In addition, they were learning how to succeed in this new land."

"But these success stories are just the foundation and are really not part of the story I want to tell you at this time. I did want to mention them now, as it does explain the origin of the success that I enjoyed here. Now, let me return to the story."

"Roland's oldest son, James, who was 24, remained in England to take care of his eventual inheritance, as I mentioned last night. The other 3 sons accompanied my great-great grandfather back to America. He did not bring along any servants or hunting dogs this time. Of these 3 sons who came with him, August, at 22, was the second oldest son. Phillip, who was to become my great-grandfather, was in the middle at 20. Clement, my namesake, was the youngest at 17."

"On this second trip, my great-great grandfather had determined that he did not want to make his way overland from the east coast to St. Louis as he had done on his first trip. This time, he would begin the trip with his sons in the port city of New Orleans and then take a steamboat up the Mississippi River and arrive at St. Louis in this manner. He had several reasons for this. One reason was that he had purchased a cotton warehouse in New Orleans on the advice of Ethan, his servant in St. Louis, and he wanted to see it. Another reason he wanted to start in New Orleans, was that he wanted to take a ride on a steamboat. He now owned a couple, and he was interested in maybe seeing them if they were in port. However, the ones he owned were really nothing more than boats built for the transportation for cargo, and although he was interested in seeing them, what he really wanted to do was to ride in a first class passenger steamboat. He wanted to make the journey as much a part of the trip as the destination this time, and see and experience different parts of America while travelling."

Again, Clem stopped his narration to include a sidebar. "I am fortunate in that a great deal of Roland's notes and the notes his sons made from this journey have survived. They are stored in dated binders in the bookcases, if you care to look through them. All I ask is that you be very careful when handling them, if you decide to look through them. I have spent a lot of time over the past years reading them and I have become so familiar with their contents that you could say I have memorized them. However, I will not attempt to relate every detail to you. If you are interested in gaining further insight about a particular time or incident, then you are welcome to refer to these binders to see if additional data is available. There is also a small notebook in the bookcases, dated 1846/7, and that is all that remains of the notes from Roland's first trip. Those notes served as the basis for the brief story you heard last night. Any questions, so far?"

Daisy raised her hand. Clem laughed and said, "I know it may feel like you are back in school and listening to a lecture, but this is not a classroom. And I apologize if I come across as if I am making you feel that it is. I am afraid that I am out of practice in entertaining, and that I may have lost the art of conversation. It is not my intent to make this a monologue with the two of you just sitting there to listen to me ramble along."

"Oh no, Clem," she responded. "If anyone has lost the art of conversation, it is Doc and I; as well as almost everyone else of our generation and younger. I only raised my hand because you looked so focused that I did not want to speak out and interrupt. I do want to clarify one point that you made, and that was, you said your ancestor was already filthy rich when he came over here with the purpose of hunting and exploring and had no intention of doing business here, right? And it was only through the decision he made to leave a servant in St. Louis, whose job it was to make preparations for his return trip and to keep his ears open to opportunity, that your great-great grandfather got involved in business here in America and made another fortune?"

"That is it exactly. You could say that it was nothing more than a random, possibly even a selfish, decision my ancestor made when he chose to leave a man behind. This man's purpose was to ensure Roland's wishes were carried out and that everything would be ready when he returned. It was only his secondary responsibility to keep his eyes and ears open to possible business opportunities, and then to simply report his findings back to Roland in England. It was the decision to give the servant that task and responsibility which led to Roland to becoming an even wealthier and more influential man. He actually became wealthy beyond even his highest expectations, and accumulated enough wealth that he was able to pass it along to all of the generations that followed."

I interrupted, "A random decision that seemed inconsequential at that moment, but which resulted in added wealth for generations of your family, and also made the servant a wealthy man. Wow, who would have believed that such a trivial decision could have such far reaching and life changing consequences for so many people?" I said in mock amazement. Then I added, "In addition, that decision had consequences that went far beyond what was originally intended, so there were intended and unintended consequences that resulted from your ancestor's choice to leave a servant behind."

She gave me a look that would wilt a head of fresh iceberg lettuce and then said, "Please don't start with the choice and consequence lecture again and ruin a good story, Doc. I guess it is a good thing that Roland picked an honest man to stay behind as his servant, who also appears to have been quite the business man himself."

Clem appreciated my point and acknowledged it by nodding to me. He pretended not to notice the look and comment she tossed at me. "Yes, Roland was very fortunate in that regard and that servant was well rewarded for his industry and honesty," Clem reminded her.

"Any other questions before I continue?" Neither of us spoke up, so Clem continued. "Since my great-great grandfather had hired a man in St. Louis to make the preparations for him, Roland was free to enjoy the trip. Also, since Roland had the foresight to ship most of their baggage and other items ahead, the three men were able to travel relatively lightly. All were looking forward to spending a few days in New Orleans, and also to seeing the country from the comfort of a steamer during the approximately 10 day trip upriver trip to St. Louis."

"Apparently, the voyage across the ocean in the sailing ship was uneventful, as the only mention of it in any of the journals was made by Phillip. Steamships were just beginning to cross the ocean and could cross it in as little as 15 days, which is blazing fast compared to the average sailing ships crossing time of 42 days, but Roland booked their passage on a sailing ship. Phillip's notes were brief but he did comment on the ' bad food, the little privacy, and the overwhelming smell of vomit and unemptied chamber pots'. In order not to be completely negative, Phillip also commented on 'the beauty and quiet of a calm sea at night when the heavens were filled from horizon to horizon with stars.' The smell of land also made quite an impression on him as well, as he stated, 'We could tell we were close to land even though none could be seen. The smell of earth and trees and flowers is something we do not notice and take for granted as land dwelling creatures. It is only when we are away from land for an extended time, and then return, that the scents overwhelm us with welcoming smells that remind us of what we have been missing.' The last mention he makes onboard the sailing ship was regarding a slave ship that his vessel overtook and passed a day or two out of New Orleans. All he said was this: "try as he might, our Captain could not get us away from the horrible odor which seemed to envelop us and the ocean in a wet pungent blanket of human waste and filth. It was only once we had passed this wretched vessel with its suffering cargo, that we could breathe freely again, although the smell seemed to have permeated everything and been absorbed by our skin.' That was their first close encounter with the peculiar institution that would soon tear the nation apart."

"Upon their arrival in New Orleans, Roland dispatched Phillip up Canal Street to find suitable lodging. August was assigned the task of overseeing the unloading of their possessions from the ship, and the re-loading of them into a carriage that would take them to whatever hotel Philip was able to find."

"While those two sons were attending to their assigned duties, Clement and my great-great grandfather walked around the wharfs and streets and did a bit of sightseeing. The wharfs and streets in New Orleans at this time were overwhelming, and at times provided unsettling experiences. There were the expected sounds and smells of a busy river port, but it was the sheer volume of commerce, and the melding of the variety of human cultures, that would dazzle the senses. There were French, English, Canadians, Americans, Spaniards, Indians, Creoles, Negroes, trappers, business men, slave traders, plantation owners, cotton traders; all shouting in their own unique dialect and with their own particular purpose. In addition, on any typical day, there were almost a hundred steamboats in the river along with several trans-ocean ships swinging at anchor, including the one on which they had just arrived. Some of the steamboats were waiting to tie up to the wharf, some were leaving the wharf, and some were tied up to the wharf and were engaged in the loading and unloading of goods and passengers. In addition, there were small boats going from shore to the ocean ships and then coming back again. Those small boats were also carrying passengers and cargo, and in some cases, slaves. The noise was almost deafening. There were voices calling back and forth to each other from boat to boat and from boat to wharf and from wharf to boat; some of these were in English and some were not. On shore, there were vendors yelling, porters loudly advertising the advantages of their hotel or restaurant, and carriage drivers vying with each other for a fare. Add to that vocal noise, the high pitched sound of boats releasing steam, the clicking sound of horse hooves and carriage wheels on the stone road and the grinding sound of wooden barrels being rolled down wooden gangplanks, and you have a variety of sounds that only a river port can produce. The air reeked of wood smoke, burning coal, river mud, human perspiration, animal sweat, excrement, urine, vomit, food cooking, tobacco smoke, stale beer, fish, and rotting vegetables. All in all, it was a lifetime of confusion and organized chaos compressed into several blocks of daily life in a southern river town."

" But it was the sounds and sights of the slaves themselves that were the most unsettling of all. Clement recorded it as a pitiful sight. Some of these poor creatures were coming to market from plantations further north. These people had been born into slavery and were accustomed to their fate. They understood what was being said and what was going to happen. They understood that they had no control and no choice over anything. These groups of slaves were chained together and made low mournful sounds as they trudged along, their feet shuffling over the cobblestone streets and their heads bowed."

"The rest of these creatures had just arrived from a slave ship. They had been taken from their homeland, crammed and packed head to toe into a ship for the last 2 or 3 months, and now unloaded into a strange place where there was nothing about their surroundings that was familiar or provided comfort. Most could not even understand what was being said to them. These groups were also chained together, but these groups did not make low mournful sounds as they shuffled through the streets. Some were in a shocked state of silence; the rest were crying, wailing, begging, and screaming. All were afraid and were trying to understand what had happened and what was going to happen; but they saw no friendly face and heard no friendly voice. They did not yet fully understand that they no longer had any control or choice in their lives."

"Then there were the sounds of the traders as they cursed their chained line of human cargo, and of their whips as they cracked the air above, getting the slaves to move along faster or to stop. The traders were careful not to let the whip touch the skin of their charges because fresh whip marks on a slave were not viewed as being good for business and did not show well on the auction block. All of these sounds mixed with the cursing and the auction itself, as the buyers yelled out their offers and the auctioneer yelled out counter offers. These sounds would then mingle with the cotton auctions going on nearby, which had its own noisy routine and cadence. On and on it went, seemingly everywhere at once. The buying, the selling, the moaning, the crying; all of this noise surrounded Clement and Roland until it seemed like the very air would break from the sound. It was the shrieks and crying of the female slaves that were the most heart rendering and unsettling noise of all. The mothers would become hysterical and fall upon their knees and beg when a child was sold, thus separating child and mother forever. When their begging was to no avail, the crying and shrieking would intensify until it reached the point of an earsplitting wail. Sometimes, the females would strike out at the trader in desperation and anger; which would only bring the sound of more curses, and the sound of more whips cracking, to an already unbearable din. Then there were the slave pens. Built of high wooden walls that would enclose an area about the size of a small house, these pens would be packed with masses of black humanity. The smell of human excrement and unwashed bodies was overpowering. It was mixed with the smell of bacon, as most of these poor souls were brought to New Orleans on the verge of starvation. Now that they were at the market place, the traders would feed them bacon and fat in order to bulk them up prior to putting them on the auction block."

"My ancestors were aware of slavery of course. They knew that slavery had been going on for time eternal. They also knew from their knowledge of European history that in the 1500's, during the wars between the Christians led by King Charles of Spain and his son Phillip against the Ottoman Turks led by the Sultan Suleiman, that slaves powered the navies of both in the Mediterranean Sea. These two warring powers each used captives from the other as slaves in their respective navies. Powering the oars for these fleets required lots of manpower, and if there were not enough captives, then each would resort to raiding sea side villages and kidnapping the inhabitants and forcing them into slavery for the navy. Roland was also aware that more Christian and Islamic slaves were taken in order to power the oars of the galleys of these two navies than African slaves had been taken to work in America to date. This was just the first time they had seen it on such an up-close and personal level. Up until now, neither of these men had formed a real negative or positive opinion on slavery. That was forever changed from this point forward."

"It turns out that things could have been a lot worse. Had they arrived a year later in the mid-summer months of July and

August, it is quite possible that some or all of my relatives would have fallen victim to the Yellow Fever Epidemic of 1853 in New Orleans and that would have been the end to my story. Over 8000 people died from that epidemic, hundreds falling victim and dying on a weekly basis from the Fever. Many were emigrates and travelers who were unaccustomed to the hot humid weather and had no immunity to the diseases brought by mosquitoes. Even for those fortunate ones who did not get sick, life during that summer was still unpleasant. In addition to watching friends and relatives die from the Fever, they had to endure the attempts by the health officials to "clear the air" of the disease. These attempts included hundreds of cannon shots, and placing barrels burning with tar all around the city. All that these attempts achieved was to make for a very noisy and smoky city that was already very noisy and smelly.."

"Now that Roland and Clement were thoroughly overwhelmed and disgusted by what they had seen, they agreed to get away from the noise and confusion of the markets and streets and head back to where they had come ashore. August should have the baggage ready by now, and then the three of them could find Phillip and check out the hotel he hopefully had found for them."

"You may remember that Canal Street was the street where Phillip was sent to find suitable lodging, while Roland and his other two sons were otherwise engaged. The name Canal Street is a bit misleading, as there is no canal on Canal Street and there never was. The street has one end anchored at the Mississippi River and the other end is anchored by the entrance to the above ground cemeteries. Cemeteries in New Orleans are above ground out of necessity. The city itself sits in a bowl that is below sea level. Any attempt to dig a grave would only result in it being filled by water as fast as it could be dug. So, the dead are entombed above ground in structures that resemble buildings along paths that resemble streets. Canal Street also marks the dividing line of the city between the original section that was populated by early French and Spanish settlers, and the newer section that began to be populated with Americans migrating to New Orleans from other parts of America after the Louisiana Purchase. There was supposed to have been a canal built here to mark this boundary and divide the two sections, and which also would have eventually connected the Mississippi River to Lake Pontchartrain. The canal was never built, but the street was named in honor of the idea of a canal. The street served as the main passageway for wagons carrying goods to and from the boats on the River and the city. It was also the main passageway for all other traffic, whether pedestrian, carriage, or riders on horseback. Free and slave."

"Phillip and August were waiting for them with a carriage and a wagon that had been loaded with their baggage. Supposedly, Clement told Phillip to take us to the hotel as soon as possible because father needed a drink. Once they checked into their separate rooms and got settled, my great-great grandfather joined the boys at the bar for a few drinks, and then he went up to his room to read and write some letters and conduct some business. He had seen enough of the streets of New Orleans during his outing earlier that day and he seldom left the hotel for the remainder of their 3 day stay. Sometimes, he joined his boys in the bar and dining room and sometimes, he took his meals and his drinks in his room. He was happy to leave the city when it was time to board their steamboat and continue their trip to St. Louis."

"The three boys, while upset by what they had seen, did not suffer from such deep feelings of despair that would keep them confined to their hotel rooms for the remainder of their stay in New Orleans. Being young men out alone in a new city, they wanted to have some fun. New Orleans had a reputation as a place where loose women, ample drink, and unlimited gambling could be found. Naturally, the three young men wanted as much of all of those things as they could find and afford, but it was Augusts' insistence that they go out and find it. The city's reputation was still true when my relatives arrived in 1852, except that the gambling houses had become more restricted. August was immediately drawn to the seedy places along the waterfront and on the edge of the Swamp, but it was

Phillip's better judgment that dictated that the boys look for their fun elsewhere. There were only a few high end gambling houses that were allowed to operate within the city limits of New Orleans, and while these houses were public, there was a certain degree of decorum that had to be followed, as not just any traveler off the street could enter. However, after a few well phrased questions and the passing of generous cash gratuities to the hotel bell staff, the boys found what they were looking for at the house located on Carondelet Street. This house catered to the wealthy, and its lavish rooms and bountiful meals were the stuff of legend. The house was also well staffed with young, beautiful, and accommodating women. The owners were well regarded by the citizens of New Orleans and they were skilled at emptying the pockets of their patrons and making their customers feel like it had been an enjoyable experience to lose their money to them. The boys found everything they were looking for here. It is needless to say, that this house is also where the boys spent the majority of their time, and a great deal of their father's money over the next 3 days."

10

Clem took a break again in his story, excused himself, and headed back towards his room to use the bathroom in order to empty out all of the old coffee he had drank. Daisy also got up and headed back to the bathroom she and I shared. Clem returned first. He settled back down into his chair, looked at the clock over the mantel, and then looked at me. "How you holding up, Doc?" he asked. "It is almost 9:00, which means we have been here for about 90 minutes, give or take. Do you and the little lady feel like listening to me for a bit longer or have you had enough for tonight?"

"I am game, and although Daisy is holding up better than she did last night, I cannot speak for her. She just went to the bathroom when you did and should be back soon. You can ask her then." Then I continued, "The description you gave of the streets and wharfs in New Orleans was very detailed. I almost felt as if I was there. All of that is written in the logs your ancestors kept? If so, then I would like to take a look later, if that is ok with you."

"Yes," he replied. "Roland kept very detailed notes of his impressions and experiences, and his sons were with him on this trip and they kept some notes as well. Not as detailed as Roland's, but they do give an added perspective from a youth's point of view that I find valuable. Like I mentioned earlier, these are all preserved in notebooks on the bookshelves and you are welcome to read through them, if you wish to. When I am speaking and telling this tale, I am also adding my own flavor and impressions to what they have written. It is unintentional, but is only natural, as I am taking what they wrote and converting it to an oral history as I tell it. It is unavoidable that I incorporate part of myself and my personality as I tell the story. This means that, by listening to me, you are hearing what they wrote, colored by my interpretation. I just hope that I do not exaggerate or minimize any portion too much. It is a shame that most his logs from his first trip to America were lost and did not survive. I imagine that those would be a priceless treasure trove of his impressions and experiences on the open prairie before that land was settled. I think that his interactions with the Indians, and all of the other men he met would make fascinating reading. So, feel free to read through what is here. I am sure you will form your own added impressions to what I said."

Daisy returned, just as I was responding to Clem by saying, "That is a good point, Clem. We appreciate your desire to remain as true as possible to what your ancestors wrote. I understand that it is only human nature that part of you becomes part of the story. Heck, you know as well as anyone that even when different people witness the exact same event at the exact same time, that these witnesses will have different and individual impressions of what they just saw. These different impressions are based in part on the different personalities and experiences of the witnesses, and these differences will convey when they relate the story to someone else."

Daisy picked up a frosted cake, examined it, looked at the clock on the mantel, shook her head slightly, and then sat the cake back onto the tray. She poured a glass of water and then asked, "Are you two going to discuss philosophy, or are we going to hear some more of the story before bed?"

"That is just what we were talking about before you entered," I responded. "You missed the first part of the conversation, and then you jumped to the assumption that we were talking philosophy," I said a little impatiently.

"Would you like to hear me talk for a little while longer, honey?" Clem asked in an attempt to diffuse the situation before it got out of hand.

"Yes, please," she stated as she settled back into her nest of pillows without looking at either of us.

And, without further ado, Clem began again.

"The morning of the men's departure from New Orleans dawned exceptionally hot and humid for late spring. Hot and humid is the norm for this city from late spring through early fall, but this morning even the longtime residents were commenting on the unusual heat. As the men began making preparations to leave the hotel, the first words out of the mouth of everyone they met, from the bell hop to the desk clerk to the carriage driver to merchants on the street, went something like: 'G'mawning genlmen. Fraid it gonna be a hot'n'.

"The typical Mississippi River steamboats were usually long wide vessels with a shallow draft and light construction. Some of them could navigate in less than two feet of water. There were 3 basic types of steam boats operating on the river at this time, and even though each type may share some characteristics of another type, the distinction remained. The first type, and the most common, was the Packet boat. The main purpose of these boats was to carry ticketed passengers, cargo, goods, and mail. Some of these steamboats had a single deck of rooms above the water line for passengers, and the rest of the space on the boat was reserved for cargo. Other steamboats had multiple decks for passengers, along with dining and saloon spaces. Some of these had the wheel along the side and some had the wheel in the stern. Naturally, there were advantages and disadvantages to each and the boat captains would have their preference of one type over the other. The steamboats with multiple passenger decks were more elaborate and catered to well-off travelers; however, they did still carry cargo, usually in reserved spaces on the bow and stern."

"The second type, and the second most common, was the Snag boat. The purpose of these boats was to remove snags and hazards from the river, thus making travel safer for other boats. These boats were the workhorses of the river and did not carry any passengers."

"The third type of boat was the showboat. These were really floating barges that looked like a long flat-roofed house on the water. The boat had a large theater for putting on the show, and the rest of the space on the boat served as the living quarters for the entertainers. These boats had no propulsion of their own and were either pushed or towed by a steamboat or a tow boat. However, they were very popular on the river, and when they passed a river town, the people would line the river bank to watch it glide by. Sometimes it would stop, and when it did, the schools would empty and the businesses would close and everyone would go to the river to observe and maybe see a show or at least an entertainer. As river travel increased and the popularity of the idea of a floating showboat gained traction, these boats also increased in demand and were very popular for several years. However, by the time of the Civil War, their popularity had begun to decline. Once the war was over, they experienced a rebirth in demand that lasted for several decades and into the turn of the century. Some of these boats evolved into floating hotels and theaters with multiple decks above the water line and were elaborately decorated both inside and out. Many now had their own propulsion but some still needed to be towed or pushed from river town to river town."

"In fact, it is rumored that the term 'highfaluting' has its origins in steamboats. The boats had high smoke stacks which terminated in fluted tops. These stacks were also called high flutes. There would normally be two of these on a boat and they would tower high over the top deck. These stacks, along with the paddle wheel and multiple stacked decks, made the steamboat easily recognizable. Since the staterooms that were located on the top deck at the base of these stacks were the most prestigious, and the most expensive rooms a passenger could book, the term highfaluting became associated with the people who travelled in these rooms because they traveled up with the high fluted stacks. So, overtime, the river people associated anyone who could afford to book a top deck room with a tendency to show off or stand out."

"As steamboat travel grew in popularity, processes began to appear in an attempt to standardize the travel for everyone. The custom developed with passenger steamboats was that the boat would arrive late at night, usually just before midnight. Another custom was that the passenger steamboat would not depart until about 17 hours later, or just before supper time of the next day. A steamboat's crew was divided into boat crew, which comprised all of the people needed to maintain and drive the boat; and the hotel crew, which comprised all of the people needed to serve and entertain the passengers. The routine was that once the boat arrived and was tied up the crew would wait for night to fall, then under cover of darkness, the designated crew would begin removing all of the trash from the voyage that was just ending and start bringing on board all the food and beverages and other supplies that would be needed for the departure voyage later that evening. At the same time, another designated crew would make any repairs the boat may need and paint any areas that needed a fresh coat. New maps and charts would also be brought on board as the river was constantly changing and even the most experienced captain wanted the most up to date information on sandbars, or any other river changes that may be documented."

"Also during this night, all passengers who were leaving the next morning would be instructed to place any baggage that they did not want to carry themselves outside their stateroom door. Around 6:00am, crew members would come around and collect the baggage and would slide a card under the stateroom door. This card would have a number and a letter printed on it. Then at 7:00am, while the departing passengers were sitting down in the dining room to a fabulous departure breakfast buffet, the baggage would be handed off to dock hands who would then assemble and secure the baggage on the dock in areas marked with brightly painted numbers and letters, which of course matched the numbers and letters on the card given to the passenger. Then when the passengers departed the boat, officers of the ship would greet them on the pier; match their passenger card to the baggage, and call for a porter who would load the baggage onto waiting carriages. It was all very efficient and graciously done. Once all passengers had disembarked, the gangplank would be secured and the cleaning and housekeeping crews would begin their tasks of cleaning all public rooms and all staterooms."

"The boarding process for new passengers began promptly at 4:00pm and would take about an hour. It was pretty much the disembarking process in reverse. Carriages would pull up on the pier with passengers and their luggage; crew would unload the baggage and escort the passengers to the room clerk and the boat's purser. These two crew members would check them in, assign the stateroom, take payment, and assign either early dinner or late dinner depending on the passenger's preference. Dinner was the only meal served in such a manner. Breakfast and lunch were served on a first come first serve basis and did not require an assigned seating time. In addition, the gambling saloon was open round the clock and food was offered there as well. Once check-in was completed, the passenger would be greeted by a bell hop who would escort them to their assigned rooms and bring the baggage. From that point on, the passengers were on left to themselves until their assigned dinner time. Most would go to the saloon to drink and gamble, the remainder would tour the boat or take a nap or write letters."

"Roland and his boys were assigned four adjacent staterooms on the upper deck. Roland's was the largest room, but all of them were well appointed and among the best rooms available. Once settled in, all 4 men headed down to the gambling saloon to have some drinks and to see if there was a poker game that they could join."

"Promptly at 6:00pm, the boat's steam whistle would give one long blast. That was the signal that the boat was about to pull away from the pier and for all people who were not crew or travelling passengers to depart the boat. Shortly thereafter, the same whistle would give several shot blasts followed by one long blast. That was the signal that all lines had been untied and the boat was now free of the pier. The boat would silently ease out into the river, and then give a slight jerk, as the big paddle wheel on the stern kicked into gear and started moving the large boat up river from New Orleans. Steam calliopes would be added in a few years and then they would be used for entertainment, as well as an additional signal to passengers and crew."

"Roland and the boys' first few days and nights on the boat went by without event. Their logs and diaries mention wonderful food in the Grand Dining Room, where the windows towered from floor to ceiling and the crystal chandeliers glowed like star points; their gambling wins and losses; remorse at the lack of single women; and how the bar at the stern of the boat, that overlooked the paddle wheel, was quickly becoming their favorite spot on the boat to pass time. They did make quite a few references to how busy the river was and several comments on how the water would sparkle during the day. At some points, the river was so wide that only one river bank could be seen and it felt as if they were back on the ocean, except that there was no wave motion. Phillip commented that, if not for the passing of the shore line, there would be no way to tell if they were actually moving. Then there were times when the river was so narrow that the tree branches from one bank would hang over the river and almost touch the tree branches from the opposite bank."

"They also mentioned the quiet dark nights when the moon would hang low over the water and the four of them would sit in cane back rocking chairs outside of Roland's stateroom and talk until late at night. They would pass other boats heading downriver from somewhere up north. The boat lights at first appeared just as twinkles on the open river and then became progressively brighter as the boats came closer. The steamboats would pass within hailing distance of each other and the men could see through the tall, brightly lit windows of the Grand Dining room and glimpse the silhouettes of those passengers on the passing boat. The sound of other boats' paddle wheel splashing through the water would mimic the sounds their own boat made. At these times, the men would get the eerie impression that they were looking at a mirror image of their own boat heading in the opposite direction. Sometimes, depending on the acoustics of the river, they could hear bits of conversations and laughter and music playing coming from the other boat as well."

"The first scheduled stop came late in the afternoon of their third day out. The boat stopped at Natchez, at the landing there call Natchez-Under-the-Hill. Natchez is located on the Mississippi side of the river, across the river from Louisiana. The boat tied up to the shore at this small town on the river to drop off two passengers, a husband and wife, who were heading back home to Natchez after visiting relatives in New Orleans; and to pick up another small group of three men heading further up river to Memphis. The disembarking and boarding process here was nothing like the one back in New Orleans. This was just a minor and short stop on the way, and because the stop would only be for a couple of hours and a handful of passengers, it did not merit the same attention as New Orleans."

"The boat tied up below towering bluffs, high up on which the main part of the town was located. Down at the base of these bluffs, by the water's edge, was the rougher and seedier part of town where saloons, gambling, and prostitutes could be found. The single street was made of dirt and mud, and was all that separated the buildings at the base of the bluff from the river bank. While the loading and unloading was going on, at the top of the river bank a small Negro slave girl, who appeared to be no more than 6 years old, stood naked and crying next to her mama. Her mama, also a slave, had an empty basket in one hand and was trying to drag the child up the street and away from the river with her other hand. Dogs and chickens ran loose on the street and outnumbered the people on the sidewalk. The sidewalk itself was made of wooden planks, which were uneven and warped. Some of the buildings, and most of the saloons, were built on stilts and these were connected to the wooden sidewalk by rickety steps. The glass windows on the buildings were open; their curtains hanging limp in the oppressive and unmoving air. Out of one of the windows, a portly working woman with pulled back blonde hair and ample bosom was eyeing the boat, as if calculating her potential for making money from any male passengers. The atmosphere of the landing and the town under the hill was one of languid licentiousness. This was exactly the type of place that appealed to August. Predictably, as soon the gangplank was lowered, he was off the boat and heading towards the attractions."

"But the area was not all as seedy as the river front section. The area was also home to many wealthy planters who owned vast tracts of land in the surrounding lowlands, on which they grew huge crops of cotton and sugar cane. Natchez gained fame as the principal river port from which these crops were exported. From here, the crops could be shipped upriver, where they made their way to Northern cities, or they could be shipped downriver to New Orleans, where they made their way overseas. This boat was not picking up any crops though, just a few passengers."

"While August was enjoying the offerings of Under-the-Hill, Roland and Clement and Phillip were having lunch with the captain of the riverboat, Captain Mike Mayweather. They had been invited to sit at the Captain's table the night before for dinner and were continuing a conversation that began then. Clement had developed quite an interest in the river, and the river boats, and wanted to know more about how they were built and navigated up and down the ever changing river. The Captain had been born on the river and learned to navigate as a youngster on flatboats and keelboats, running cargo up and down the river. He started working on steamboats in his mid-twenties and now had 20 years of experience on various steamboats of all types and sizes. Captain Mayweather said that he knew of only two types of people who would come to work on the river. The first type worked the river because they loved it and working the river was a pleasure to them. The river would become their mistress. The other type worked the river in order to heal a deep hurt and working the river was a balm to them. The river would become their nurse until they healed."

"Mayweather had been aboard this steamboat for the last 3 years and was its first and so far it's only captain. During lunch, Clement began to pepper the captain with so many questions that Roland felt compelled to interfere and apologize for his youngest son's rude behavior. The Captain waved off Roland's apology, as he thought curiosity was a good thing for a boy to have. He then told Clement that he was mighty fond of the strawberry ice cream that the galley kitchen made once a week, but that as a member of the ship's crew, he was not allowed to have more than a small taste. However, as a passenger, and one of the youngest ones at that, Clement could get all he wanted. The Captain made a deal that if Clement would bring a large bowl of strawberry ice cream up to him in the pilot house just after sunset that evening, then the Captain would teach Clement river navigation and chart reading, and maybe even let him steer the boat. The arrangement would remain in effect for the rest of the trip, so that whenever Clement wanted a lesson all he had to do was show up in the pilot house at sunset with a large bowl of strawberry ice cream. As a result, Clement spent a least a couple of hours each evening in the pilot house with the Captain, absorbing everything like a sponge."

Clem paused here for a minute and said, "I am getting ahead of myself here in the story a little, but this is the perfect place for me stop the story for a minute or two and finish talking about Clement. As I told you earlier, I was named after him and he was the youngest of Roland's children at 17. It turned out that Clement actually had a knack for riverboat navigation and caught on very quickly. When the group reached St. Louis, the Captain asked if he would like to remain on the boat as his apprentice and possibly one day be captain of his own boat. Clement was overjoyed and it was obvious to everyone that he loved the river. Roland recognized this and agreed to the Captain's offer, on the condition that Clement could rejoin him or return to England at any time, if things did not work out. Clement stayed with Captain Mayweather for the next 2 years, and became the captain of his own boat in the 3rd year. He led a very happy life, married a pretty young girl from Baton Rouge, and captained his own boat carrying passengers from New Orleans to Memphis and St. Louis. He did this up until the Civil War. The war of course had a negative impact on river transport; and normal business commerce and travelling were disrupted. Clement tried to remain neutral but shortly after the war started, with business drying up and his funds diminishing, he made the choice to start carrying soldiers and war materials for the Confederacy to various points up and down the river. He was a brave man and made many friends among the southern soldiers and citizens along the river towns. He was fearless in his belief that the supplies he was delivering would save lives, and he was determined to deliver his cargo safely. He continued doing this until he was killed during the siege of Vicksburg in June of 1863 at age 28. He was running food and medical supplies into that surrounded city, when his boat was blown apart by a Union artillery shell. It was considered a good death. He was well known and liked by many of the town citizens, and when they found his body the next day they buried him in the cemetery there in town. The few possessions of his that were recovered were sent back to his wife in Baton Rouge, and she then forwarded most of them to his older brother at the family estate back in England. A few remained in the family and were passed down but most became lost over time. In the tall bookcase, by the fireplace, are his Captain's license dated 1856 and his snuff box."

Clem paused again here. He walked over to the bookcase and motioned for us to join him. He swung out the glass door of the second shelf up from the bottom. The glass of the door sparkled and there was no dust either on it or in the case. I thought to ask him how he kept it so clean but then I dismissed the thought as unimportant. From inside the case, he picked up a small gilded picture frame which contained Clements's license for us to see. It was dated June 28, 1856 and stamped with the seal of City of New Orleans, Louisiana River Navigation Authority, and was signed by Captain Mayweather and witnessed by two other city officials.

"Do you have a picture of him?" Daisy asked.

"No, unfortunately not," Clem replied. "In later years, the license would have a picture attached to it, but back then all that was provided was a printed and stamped license." He then handed up the snuff box, which was made of walnut, with an ivory inlaid top that had the profile of a steamboat etched on it. The top flipped open on a hinge, and when opened an engraving on the inside that read 'Happy Birthday, your loving wife', could be viewed.

"It is lovely," Daisy said. Then she added, "So sad too. What happened to her?"

"Who?" Clem asked.

"His wife of course," she replied.

"Oh, she never remarried. She inherited some money from her father-in-law's estate when Clement was killed, so she was financially comfortable. However, she was not physically well off. She suffered from depression and was stricken with polio soon after and lived another 30 years as a cripple. There was one child, a girl named Hibernia. She was just a toddler when her father was killed. She never married but spent her life taking care of her mother and teaching school in Baton Rouge. When her mother died, Hibernia thought the gravesite looked lonely, so she had a head marker with her father's name placed next to her mother's grave. Remember that her father was buried in Vicksburg, but she did not want to move his body. However, she did want some remembrance of him close to her mother's final resting place. When Hibernia died, she was buried there as well, next to her mother."

As he placed these items back, he asked if we were ready to hear some more of his family story or had we heard enough? We both answered that we were ready to hear more.

"So, where was I?" Clem asked once we all had reclaimed our seats.

"August was exploring the sights of Natchez while your other 3 ancestors had lunch with the boat captain," Daisy answered.

"Oh yes, thank you" Clem responded. He then continued, "The boat was scheduled to depart Natchez around sunset, after having stopped there for only a few hours. Just as Roland was about to send Phillip out to look for him, August came stumbling drunk down the riverbank and managed to cross the gangplank, with some assistance from Phillip and one of the deck hands. He was singing happily and apparently had a grand time under the hill. Phillip quieted him and then escorted him down the side of the boat to the outdoor staircases, hoping in this way to disturb and be observed by as few passengers as possible. Once in Augusts' room, Roland joined them and August proceeded to relate his adventure. His wallet was several hundred dollars lighter now but he said that it was well worth the cost. The gambling houses were crap and not worth the cost, because August believed that they were rigged and survived only by cheating. However, the money he had generously spent on liquor, and on two very enticing and well-endowed prostitutes, more than made up for the gambling and worth every dollar. 'Under-the-Hill was truly an evil place' he slurred 'but worth another visit, one day'. With that, Phillip pushed August back onto the bed where he was soon snoring and where he stayed for rest of the evening."

"The boat steamed on through the night, without incident, was scheduled to arrive in Vicksburg the next morning, around 8:00am. While August was quiet in his room, Roland and Phillip decided to head down to dinner. Clement had eaten earlier and was already up in the pilot house with his ice cream bribe for the captain. After dinner, Roland and Phillip spent some time gambling in the saloon with some acquaintances they had met the first night in New Orleans along with the three new passengers who had just joined the boat in Natchez. After a couple of hours of trading money back and forth with the other men at the table, our two men had enough and headed upstairs to their rooms. They wrote that they could hear August snoring as they sat outside in the rocking chairs and watched the river float by."

"Some sections of the river are lined with cotton fields that stretch along the bank for miles and as far inland as the men on the boat can see. Sometimes, the grand plantation house can be seen and some of these plantations have their own well-built wharfs where a steamboat can moor and cotton can be loaded onto the boat by the slaves without having to transport it to a town. This makes transporting the cotton overland to a river port like Natchez unnecessary, thus saving the planter both time and money. The section of river between Natchez and

Vicksburg that the men were on this night was a particularly quiet section where both banks of the river were lined with forest. The men would comment several times on how the river would go from passing through a forest, to passing through immense fields, to passing through small towns and larger ones. Tonight, as they glided through the forest, the only sounds that could be heard other than the splash of the paddle wheel were frogs croaking, crickets chirping, and an occasional alligator bellow. When close enough to shore, the men could see the eyes of these beasts reflecting in the light from the boat. They were eerily luminescent, fiery orbs that did not blink, and only disappeared when the creature grew bored and submerged. The dancing of fire flies was another frequent sight, as thousands of these insects would light up a field or a forest with their blinking signals. Roland commented that night on the river was like riding through a muggy black velvet tunnel, enclosed with a roof of stars and clouds, and the sides lined with the sounds and lights made by the mysterious and shy creatures that owned the river; and who grudgingly allowed us to pass though their domain. He loved it."

"And although he did not know it, he now owned some of these lands that he was passing through on his way to St. Louis. As mentioned earlier, his man in St. Louis had been quietly and selectively making purchases. Roland would not own any plantation lands, as those could not be purchased at this time. After the war, some could be had for the taxes owed, but Roland's man had being buying undeveloped timber land along the river that bordered the small and larger towns, knowing that these towns would grow as river travel and rail travel grew; and as the towns grew, the land value would also grow. Turns out that Roland was quite the landowner himself, he just did not know it yet."

"The boat arrived in Vicksburg on schedule the next morning at 8:00am. This was the last scheduled stop before the boat's scheduled arrival in Memphis two days later. Vicksburg is another river city that was built up on high bluffs overlooking the river. However, the riverfront here was tame compared to Natchez and most other river ports. The townsfolk in Vicksburg had expelled all professional gamblers 17 years prior, in 1835, due to rumor that these gamblers supported a plot by abolitionist John Murrell. Five gamblers refused to leave and were hung. A respected town doctor was shot, and ever since then, the few remaining gamblers in the city kept a much lower profile. Although tensions had been rising steadily over the slavery issue since those days, no one could have foreseen the fact that the city would lie in ruins 11 years hence and its inhabitants starved and bombarded into submission."

"The men stayed on the boat during the 5 hours it was docked in Vicksburg. Phillip and Roland were writing letters and August was not quite ready for another round of drinking, gambling, and womanizing just yet. Clement was up with the captain, fascinated to learn that there are actually two rivers around Vicksburg. The Yazoo River parallels the Mississippi here and then joins it just north of the city. The boat tied up to a pier on the Yazoo River since there was no berth available on the Mississippi."

Clem paused again for a minute. He stretched his leg and his arms and started to pour himself another cup of coffee. Daisy was relaxed and awake in her nest of pillows on the couch. I was very comfortable in the red leather chair with my feet propped up on a matching leather ottoman. Clem was smiling at us and holding the coffee pot in mid-air, as if trying to decide whether to tip the pot just a bit more and pour the coffee into his cup, or whether to angle the pot back to vertical and set it down on the table. He finally made up his mind and poured himself another cup. Without speaking, he offered some to us by pointing the spout of the coffee pot at our coffee cups and making a slight pouring motion with his arm and hand. We each declined by shaking our head and covering our coffee cups with our hands. Clem returned to his seat and then spoke, "I know it is getting late, but there are two more things that happened on the boat trip to St. Louis that I want to tell you about. The reason I want to tell you about these two events is because, if they had not occurred, then the trip up river would be pretty much a repeat of what you have heard so far. Travelling on the river could be peaceful and it was a wonderful way to travel in comfort then as well as now, but it can become monotonous. So, if you two can bear with me for just a little longer then I will stop and we can go to bed."

"I am fine with that," Daisy said.

"Me too," I responded. Then I asked, "About how much longer do you think you will need tonight, Clem?"

"I would like to tell you about a storm the men experienced on the river and then a story about August. So, about another hour, give or take," he said.

"Well, in that case, I will have another cup of that coffee," I said as I lifted my feet off of the ottoman and leaned forward to retrieve the pot from the table.

As I poured myself a fresh cup, Clem began. "The boat left Vicksburg as scheduled at 1:00 that afternoon. It was now on a 2 day non-stop scheduled run to Memphis, and then from Memphis, the boat would complete the final 3 days to St. Louis with possible brief stops in New Madrid and Cape Girardeau, both small river towns along the Missouri shore."

"The day had once again dawned hot and muggy. The humidity increased dramatically as the day wore on and the heat continued to build. By the time the boat left Vicksburg, dark billowing clouds were observed to the west. Standing in the pilot house, the captain cast a wary eye towards them, but he was an experienced boat man and not prone to over-worry or becoming unnecessarily concerned. Besides, he had a schedule to keep."

"Three hours later, the captain became concerned. The boat was now about 22 miles north of Vicksburg and the wind had picked up considerably, enough in fact, to make small whitecaps on the usual smooth surface of the river. Looking towards the shore, the tops of the trees could be seen swaying and bending as the wind whipped through them. Sunset was still several hours away, but the clouds had darkened the sky so much that it resembled twilight. Lightening could be seen flashing across the dark sky in streaks that ran horizontal to the ground. These flashes would be followed soon after by thunder claps that would build from a low rumble and then break and roll across the sky and echo off of the water. The captain ordered lookouts to the bow of the boat and to the upper deck, to scan the shore for a suitable place to land. The section of the river they were now travelling through was heavily forested on both banks with trees that came right down to the water's edge. This was an advantage, but it was also a disadvantage. The spot the captain was looking for would ideally have steep banks for protection and be surrounded by trees large enough for him to securely tie his boat too. The fact that both banks were heavily forested also meant that no one lived nearby, and that he would not be able to count on any help from landowners if the boat got into serious trouble."

"The captain knew all sections of the river as well as he knew the layout of his own house, and he knew that the banks along the shore were not steep here. He also knew that he was quickly running out of time. He still needed to land the boat and then still have enough time to send his crew out to securely tie her before the storm fully hit. After searching over a mile of riverbank, he settled on a spot that was in a bend of the river and had large trees right down to the water line. Since there were no banks, at least the river bend would provide some additional protection. By now, the rain had started to fall in wind swept sheets that only made a bad situation worse. Visibility had decreased to only a few yards and the shrieking wind made it almost impossible for the captain, or anyone, to be heard. A messenger was sent to request the assistance of all male passengers in getting the boat safely moored to the trees. Clement, of course, had been on deck since departing Vicksburg and now he was joined by his brothers and his father as well as every other man aboard. The captain ordered that strong ropes be run from 3 spots on the boat to the strongest trees available on land. He had rope tied off to stanchions on the bow, amidships, and the stern. He placed men at these points, to pass the other end of the rope to men who were in the water, and who would swim the short distance to shore. Once ashore, these men would wrap their end of the rope around the thickest trees they could find, taking as much of the slack out of the rope as they could. Then, they would tie and secure their end. The captain had the anchor lowered for additional stability as well. The work went well and it went quickly. Within 30 minutes of picking the spot, the boat was tied off and secured. The only thing left to do now was ride out the storm and hope that none of these trees would be struck by lightning or toppled by the wind and crush the boat."

"The lightning was no longer horizontal; it was now breaking the darkness in vertical streaks that ran from cloud to ground. The thunder crashed almost simultaneously with the lightning flashes, adding its own ear splitting booms that shook the entire boat and caused the men to pull their heads down closer to their body. The storm was right on top of the boat and it raged for hours. Trees could be heard moaning, and sometimes, snapping. The captain stayed on deck the entire time, checking the ropes and his position, to make sure the boat was not drifting or sinking. He sent all of the men, except for his crew, back to their cabins for safety purposes. He also told them to remain sober, in case they were needed again. As a precaution, he had the saloon closed. Finally, around 9:00pm, the storm began to subside. The rain remained for a couple of more hours, sometimes falling heavily, but not in sheets like before. The wind, thunder, and lightning moved off completely an hour later. After the rain stopped, it became very quiet along the river as if it were resting after an intense physical ordeal. A low fog moved in and covered the river and the shore and the boat in a soft blanket. Water could be heard dripping from the trees and the river could be heard sloshing against the side of the boat. Roland and Clement stood on deck and listened and observed as this change came over the river. Also, now that the storm was gone, the animals in the forest and the alligators in the water began to stir again. The animals could be heard moving about and the alligators could be heard moving through the water between the boat and the shore. Every now and then, their eyes would catch a ray of light and reflect it back to the men standing by the boat rail. Eventually, the men went to bed. The captain decided to keep the boat tied to the tree until daylight because he was sure the river would be full of debris caused by such a furious storm and it would be better for all if that debris could be seen and avoided."

"The next morning dawned quiet and calm. The passengers came on deck to observe the damage. The boat suffered minor damages to the upper decks and quite a bit of broken glass, but nothing that would affect her ability to continue steaming up river. This boat did not have all of the necessary materials to make the repairs, but these could be repaired when they reached Memphis. The trees along some sections of the shore line did not fare as well. Once the boat was back into the river and underway again, the true strength of the storm could be seen. There were long stretches where most of the trees had been broken and uprooted, along the shore and as far inland as could be seen. Then, there would be sections where the damage was less. The place the captain had chosen along the bend was one of those places where the damage was considerably less. It became apparent to everyone just how fortunate and lucky they had been. That night at dinner, the captain was treated to a standing ovation and 3 hearty cheers of hip-hip-hooray. In acknowledgement of the appreciation and assistance of the passengers during the storm, the captain ordered that all bar drinks be served on the house for the rest of the evening. After dinner, all 4 men stayed late in the saloon, each playing at separate tables of poker. This was the first time the men had played poker with the 3 new passengers from Natchez. Roland took an immediate dislike to all three. He did not record a specific reason for his dislike, other than where he characterized the 3 men 'as belonging to the lowest caliber of riverboat gambler, as these men are both shady in their demeanor and crass in their conversation'."

"The captain had lost over 12 hours of steaming time, while riding out the storm. Under normal circumstances, he would be able to make up a few hours of that time; however, he was not so confident that he could make up any time on this trip. One of his concerns was the condition of the river after the storm. He was afraid that channels could have changed slightly, and it is possible that sandbars could have moved or new ones created, and certainly there would be new snags to watch out for, and it was guaranteed that there would be floating debris to lookout for. Another of his concerns was the possibility that he would encounter other boats where the people had not been as fortunate as he had been. It was quite likely he would come across a wrecked steamboat where he would be called upon to assist, and possibly provide medical aide to their passengers and crew. It was also equally possible that he would come upon a wrecked home or plantation, whose inhabitants also needed assistance."

"However, the captain was wrong on all of his concerns. As the boat steamed further north passing forests, and an occasional cotton field, the damage from the storm became less. After an hour of slow steaming, in which time the boat had travelled about 4 miles, there was no more storm damage. Obviously, the captain had no idea how much damage had been done further south or even inland, but apparently, the storm had been confined to a relatively small stretch of river, north of where he tied up. This was good news and the boat was able to increase its speed and try to make up a few hours of lost time. The boat arrived in Memphis at 5:00pm, only 9 hours behind schedule. The repairs were set to begin almost immediately, in hopes that the boat could still reach its destination of St. Louis on schedule in 3 days."

"The boat tied up along the waterfront in Memphis, near where the western end of Beale Avenue, later Beale Street, terminated at the Mississippi River. The western end of the street was where the merchants, who traded goods with the river boats, were located. The eastern end of the street was lined with houses. In between these two ends were the saloons, gambling halls, and other forms of the usual entertainment. Since the boat would be here overnight, all 4 men decided to take a look around. I think Roland went along mainly to keep an eye on August, who had a tendency to overindulge, as we have seen."

"Memphis was also a major slave market. After their exposure to the workings of this type of market in New Orleans, the men avoided these sections in Memphis. However, there was one thing that Roland was interested in seeing and learning more about and that was the railroad. His man in St. Louis had written him about plans for a railroad that would be the first to link the Atlantic Ocean to the Mississippi River. Construction had already begun, and would be completed in just a few years. Some of the railroad would be new construction, and parts of the railroad would incorporate already existing smaller lines. The line began in Memphis and would run to Charleston, SC. When completed, it would be called the Memphis and Charleston Railroad. Roland's man had already purchased land along its proposed route, and had several other pieces of land under negotiation. This rail line did very well and prospered until the Civil War. What had been an advantage in peacetime became a disadvantage in war. This railroad had the unfortunate distinction of being the only East-West rail link across the Confederacy, and as a result, it received a lot of focus and attention from the Union army. After the War, this line, like all of the rail lines, lay in a state of devastation. Most were rebuilt, repaired and operated again. The Memphis and Charleston Railroad was eventually consolidated with several other rail lines and became the Southern Railway System, under the control of J. P. Morgan in the late 1890's."

"About a dozen passengers disembarked from the boat in Memphis, upon arrival. The next day, about the same number of passengers boarded, all of them bound for St. Louis. The departing group primarily consisted of couples, husbands and wives on their way home from visiting New Orleans. The arriving group primarily consisted of single men heading to St. Louis, and was a mixture of businessmen and gamblers. Both groups arrived and departed without fanfare, due to the boat's late arrival and the repair work going on to fix the damage, particularly the broken glass in the stateroom windows."

"Shortly after noon on the day after arrival in Memphis, the boat cast off from the dock and began its final leg of the journey to St. Louis. The men had experienced quite a bit of Southern river life in the 3 previous towns the boat had visited; New Orleans, Natchez, and Memphis. The boat had also stopped in Vicksburg but none of the men left the boat during that stop. Unfortunately, they really had not explored more than a couple of blocks from the river in any of these towns, and since this was their very first visit to towns in the Southern states, they had no other experiences of Southern life to weigh these river town experiences against. So, it was easy and natural for them to take what they had seen along the riverfront and apply it to life in the South in general. They assumed that every Southern town had a market where slave auctions were held daily, and every town's business section consisted of cotton merchants, sugar merchants, and bankers, and that every town had a section of saloons, gambling houses, and prostitutes. They also assumed that all planters lived in mansions, on huge plantations, and owned a small army of slaves. I only mention this because Phillip and Roland recognized and wrote about the mistake of their assumption years later, in their journals. Clement never acknowledged his mistake, probably because, as already mentioned, he never left the South or the River. He died there several years later. August never mentioned it because of what I am going to tell you next."

"August was the largest of all of Roland's sons, but not an overweight out-of-shape type of large. He was a tall and muscular man and well-proportioned. He had clear blue eyes, sandy hair, and an easy smile. Back in England, he had been the county champion boxer for 5 years in a row. As with many big men, his size was a curse, and made him a constant target for other men who felt the need to prove themselves against a bigger man. Augusts' personality was such that he ignored these challenges, as far as it was possible to do so. He had the reputation among his friends and family as being a man who did not start fights, he just finished them. As you have probably gathered so far, he loved to socialize and to gamble and to drink. He did have a bit of a dark side. He particularly liked, and was drawn to, the seedier parts of any town and to the men and women who could be found there. This feature of his personality had been a source of embarrassment to Roland back in England, but here in America, no one really seemed to notice or care. In fact, August seemed more at home and comfortable here in America than he ever had back in England, but this dark side of August was a source of concern to Roland.

Madness and depression were traits that ran in the family, and Roland thought he could see the glimmerings of that trait in Augusts' attraction with depravity and the baser side of life."

"Almost every steamboat paddle wheeler on the Mississippi River at that time was known for its card games and for the gamblers who rode them, many of whom made their living by preying on the river boat travelers. This steamboat was no different, and carried its share of these men. Roland and his boys had met several of these men over poker games in the saloon, where everyone had won and lost and the boys were basically trading money back and forth in harmless games. Even though Roland did not like the men who had boarded in Natchez, there had been no trouble from them. August was most familiar with these men, as he spent more time than the others gambling. After departing Memphis, the saloon soon became crowded with men who had nothing better to do for the next 3 days but drink and gamble. The saloon was relatively small, but there was space enough for a standing bar and for 4 tables in the smoke filled room. Each table had a limit of 5 men that could play at a time. The floor was of highly polished and varnished wooden planks. This was unlike the other public rooms and the staterooms, where the floors were covered in plush carpet. The chairs around the tables were also of wood, short with wrap around backs and armrests. The lighting was provided by oil lamps, one of which sat in the middle of each wooden felt covered table. The others hung from hooks on the walls and served as primitive sconces. There was no enforced dress code; but all of the men wore some combination of vest and jacket, cotton shirt, puff tie, dress woolen pants, and boots. The gamblers usually had the brightest colored vests with Red Rosebarr, Golden Thistle, or Peacock Blue being the most popular vest colors. Guns and knives were carried by everyone, but were not always visible. Hats of all types were worn by all. The best dressed gamblers would wear a variation of a stove pipe, but most passengers simply wore either short brim Pinkerton style hat or a wide brim modified cavalry type of hat."

"August got into a card game shortly after the boat left Memphis, and he was still playing when Roland and Phillip called it quits around 11:00pm and headed up to their staterooms. Clement was in the pilot house with the captain, as usual. The night was calm, but pitch dark as there was no moon. Clement wanted to experience piloting the boat on a night like this and the captain had allowed him to stay. Actually, Clement was now spending more time in the pilot house than he was spending with his father and brothers. Roland glanced back over his shoulder as he exited the saloon, just as August raised his eyes from his cards. Their eyes met, and August winked at Roland as he pushed a large stack of chips to the center of the table. That would be the memory Roland kept of August, as it was the last time he saw him. He always regretted his decision to leave, thinking that if he had stayed a little longer, then maybe August would still be alive."

According to the captain's report, August left the saloon alone around between 2:30am and 3:00am. No one was observed to have followed him, and as far as anyone knew, the only people awake on the boat at that time were the people in the saloon and whatever boat's crew would have been up at that hour. August exited the saloon and turned left; heading aft towards the stairs that led to the upper deck staterooms. The bartender and other gamblers said that he was very drunk. He was so drunk, in fact, that he left his winnings on the table and did not take them when he left. His winnings were counted out to be over five hundred dollars, which the bartender collected after August left, and put the money in the cash box behind the bar for safe keeping. He had two of the other gamblers sign a receipt witnessing and confirming the amount."

"No one even knew August was missing until later that morning, around 11:00, when Phillip knocked on Augusts' stateroom door. When there was no answer, he entered and found the room had not been used the night before. The bed was untouched and Augusts' night clothes were laid out over the bed, untouched as well. Phillip immediately went to his father who in turn went to the captain. A search of the boat was conducted, but nothing was found."

"Augusts' body was never found either, and he was presumed to have accidently fallen overboard and drowned. Remember, that although the river was calm, it was a very dark night with no moon, and August was quite intoxicated. Bad things happen to good people all of the time and the matter was never fully investigated. There was no real law and no one to do any real investigation anyway. Besides, no one really cared; it was just one of those unfortunate things that happen to people in the West. Everyone tended to believe that it was nothing more than an unfortunate accident. According to the report, and as I already said, August never removed his winnings from the card table when he got up to leave. He certainly did not need the money, as he had hunting dogs that were worth more than his poker winnings that night. Five hundred dollars was pocket change to him and to the family. However, money is money and August would not have just left that much money if he had been in his right mind. He did enjoy the gambling for the sport of it, but he also enjoyed winning and being able to brag about it to his brothers. Also, the fact that he did not have his winnings on him, as everyone observed, means that there was really no reason for anyone to kill him for robbery because he was not carrying the winnings. Maybe one of the other gamblers was upset that this kid had embarrassed him in poker and arranged to have him thrown overboard, but no one really believed that. In any event, we'll never know. My great-great grandfather did meet with the riverboat captain and the captain referred to his maps and charts and was able to determine approximately where on the river the boat was at the time his August left the saloon."

"The boat was not scheduled to make any more stops before St. Louis, but the captain broke this rule and stopped in the next town, which was New Madrid, MO. He and Roland made a report to the local authorities, just in case August had survived and found his way to the town. Then the captain and Roland borrowed some horses and rode out back downriver to the nearest plantation. Here they met with the plantation owner and his overseer. They explained what had happened and Roland offered the owner payment if he would have his slaves search the river banks for his son's body, or even some of his belongings. The owner agreed to search, but refused payment saying that it was his duty and honor to help. He also said, that if Augusts' body was found, he would see to it that a message was sent to Roland's son, Clement, who would be staying and working on the riverboat. He also promised that Augusts' body would be given a proper Christian burial, but nothing was ever found of August. The river runs deep and swift through this area and could have carried August's body many miles downriver from where he fell over. If his body was carried far enough down river, then his corpse could have become food. Alligators need to eat too."

"So, the now three men continued their journey to St. Louis. As you can imagine, the remaining two days were somber for everyone; particularly for the family of course, but also for the other passengers and crew who had met and come to know August. His quick smile and fun loving ways had endeared him to many. Roland spent most of the remaining time on board taking inventory and carefully packing Augusts' belongings. When the boat reached St. Louis, and once again docked at Laclede's Landing, Roland placed these belongings in the care of Clement and Captain Mayweather. The boat would be leaving and returning to New Orleans in a couple of days. Roland's instructions were to ship Augusts' belongings back to England once they reached New Orleans. My great-great grandfather also requested that Captain Mayweather place a brass plaque with Augusts' name at the ship's bar. They all agreed that would be a fitting memorial to August, and one that he would approve of. Phillip jokingly added that maybe they should put a plaque in Natchez as well, in the room August had shared with the two prostitutes just a few days prior. This brought a great laugh and head nods to the men, as an acknowledgement to an appropriate joke. Once ashore, Roland met his servant Ethan and conveyed the sad news. Roland's servant had known all of Roland's sons since birth and he was quite overcome with this news. The next day, without asking approval, Ethan found and commissioned a stone mason to carve a four foot tall marble memorial obelisk to Augusts' memory. It would simply be engraved with Augusts' name and the line 'Drowned near here, 1852.' He also arranged, that once it was completed, that it would be loaded on a steamboat and taken downriver to New Madrid. From there, it would be loaded onto a wagon and carried over rutted roads to a small parcel of land along the river, near where it was thought August fell overboard and met his death. There, it would be erected. The mason estimated that he could do the carving in six months. Ethan told him that was unsatisfactory and that he would triple the mason's fee if it could be done in 30 days, upon which it was agreed and a down payment was made. When the servant told Roland and Phillip of this, both were grateful beyond words. All of these things eased Roland's mind, and with that, they disembarked and continued their journey. He knew that he had done all he could to honor Augusts' memory."

"Safety was more of a theory than a practice on most riverboats in those days. Grounding accidents, collisions, boiler explosions, and fires were regular occurrences on the river. Captain Mayweather was an exception, in that he took the safety of his passengers and his boat seriously. He and Clement served on the same boat together for the next two years. Then, Captain Mayweather retired and Clement went on to captain his own boat. After the Captain retired, the boat that had brought Clement and his family to St. Louis continued to carry goods and passengers up and down the river from St. Louis to New Orleans. However, the boat was getting older and the new captain was not as safety minded, and one bright spring morning just downriver from Helena, Arkansas, the boiler on the steamboat exploded and completely destroyed the vessel, killing everyone onboard. Clement wrote his father that for several years thereafter, during the dry season when the river ran low, the keel of the boat could be seen resting in the mud, but that is all that remained of her. Just a few years after that, heavy rains caused massive flooding all along the plains of the Mississippi River. The marble obelisk that marked the area where August drowned was washed away and was never recovered. That erased the last tangible link to the memory of August, and it was as if he had never stepped foot in America.

Outside of his brothers and his father and the handful of people on the boat, there was no one else in America who knew August. His immediate family would remember August until the day they died, of course. Their memory of him would fade over time; and their thoughts of him would become less frequent as time passed, but his memory would remain as long as his family lived. The other people on the boat would only remember August as the hard drinking gambler, who fell overboard and drowned in the Mississippi River, somewhere between New Orleans and St. Louis. Only a short time would pass before there would be no one who could recall August. No one to remember how strong and easy going he was, or how his eyes would twinkle when he smiled, or how he was attracted to the seedier parts of a town, or how he blew a pile of money on two prostitutes in a rigged poker game in Natchez, Mississippi. Those stories would soon never be told again. He now truly joined the ranks of those who were gone and forgotten."

"St. Louis was a bustling river city in 1846, when Roland first visited it. Now, six years later, it was even more so. Well over one hundred steamboats of all types and sizes lined the shore or were sitting out in the river. The river front itself had changed, and it reminded Roland more of the New Orleans he had left just over a week ago than of the St. Louis he remembered from six years ago. The commerce was still brisk and the excitement of being on the edge of the frontier was still present, but there was a perceptible change in atmosphere and in the attitude of the people that Roland sensed and recognized immediately. The Mexican-American War was just beginning when he was last here. Now, the westward expansion that the winning of that war allowed was in full swing, and with that expansion, a new tension in the air had moved in and overtaken the passions of many Americans. Like New Orleans, and the other river cities, the people saw their future as being tied to commerce on the river, particularly the sugar and cotton commerce. Now, that vision of what the future held was increasingly uncertain. Although Missouri was a slave state, Roland felt more of the uncertainty here than he had down south. The reason for this uncertainty, was that the cotton and sugar commerce rested on the labor of slaves, and while some could overlook the continuation of that system for the time being, the question of the expansion of slavery was becoming more openly discussed; and that openness was more apparent here in St. Louis than it had been in New Orleans; and as that discussion was more openly discussed, it was also becoming more and more heated, as both sides attempted to rally supporters to their side in order to make their point the dominant one. Two years prior, The Compromise of 1850 had been passed and it was holding a lid on things for now, but the pot was starting to boil and would soon boil over. In two more years, the Kansas-Nebraska Act of 1854 was passed and it virtually guaranteed civil war."

Clem abruptly stopped talking and we both looked over at him. He just sat there in his chair with a strange look on his face, as if he had actually experienced, and was reliving, some portion of the events he had just told us. He looked haggard and drawn. The bags under his eyes seemed to have gotten deeper and darker since the last break in his story. His eyes looked even more liquid and translucent. His body shuddered with a sigh that seemed to well up from some hidden place, deep within his soul. Then, very softly, he said, 'The Civil War left a deep oozing scar on this country that is very similar to the deep oozing scar that I carry in my soul." Then, he fell silent again, with his chin resting on his chest.

I thought maybe he had died and was just about to ask him if he was ok, when he spoke, "Well, I promised the two of you that we would quit for the night once I told you about the storm and about August. I am now finished with those two stories and I am pretty tired. I thought it would take me about an hour to tell these things and I see by the clock that I went a little over. It is now well after midnight, it is actually 1:15am, do you mind if we call it a night? I am almost completely finished with the entire story and I promise that I will finish it tomorrow. I have told you this much of my family story, and I feel I should complete it by letting you know what eventually happened to Roland and Phillip. Plus, I promised Doc that I would tell him how I came from running a prosperous ranch and farm to the state you see me in now. Then, once I finish, I will have only one more favor to ask and then the two of you can be on your way. I am not trying to rush you away, in fact I would love it if you stayed, but that seems impossible now. I know you both need to get back and I feel that our time is coming to an end."

It was with some effort that I pushed myself up out of the chair. My knee was a great deal better but sharp pains would still radiate from it if I went from an inactive state to an active state too quickly. Once I got to my feet, I held out my hand to help Daisy up from her nest on the couch, and then I helped Clem to his foot. While he turned down the lights, Daisy and I picked up the coffee pot and water pitcher and all of the dirty glasses, and cups, and other things and took them to the kitchen. We were setting them in the sink basin when Clem passed by us on his way to his room. He got to the door that led to his room, and just as his hand was turning the door knob, he turned around toward us, "Do either of you need anything?" he asked.

I shook my head and Daisy said, "I think we are good, Clem."

"Goodnight then, I will see you tomorrow for breakfast," he said. Then added, "Daisy, do you think you can whip up another breakfast like you did this morning? It was the best I have had in a very long time."

"You got it, Clem," she said. "I know where everything is now. Around 8:30 be ok?"

"That will be perfect, honey," he said as he closed the door.

I had started washing the dishes, instead of just leaving them there for the morning. Daisy walked over close to me, and then leaned in and kissed me on the cheek. "You are a good man, Doc," she said. I am sorry if I have been a bit short these last couple of days. These events have given me a lot to think about, and I know things have been distant and strained between us these past few days. I hope the distance will go away and that we'll be close again soon, but tonight I am pretty tired. I think these bee stings took a larger toll on us than we realized. I am going back to bed now, but I will see you in the morning."

With that, she gave me another kiss on the cheek and disappeared around the corner, and I was left to wash and dry the dishes alone. At least I knew that there was now no point in knocking on her door when I did head back that way, but I also knew that the possibility existed that tomorrow night could be different. I finished the last of the dishes with a grin on my face.

11

I stopped in the family room on my way back to the room I was sleeping in. Clem had turned all the lamps off, except one that cast a warm glow in the center of the room. I stood there for a few minutes, just listening to the clocks tick in that half-light. The glass on the cases reflected back the light from the lamp and the shapes and shadows created by the furniture. I walked over to the guns that were hanging over the mantel and examined the ones that were displayed there. Some of these guns were muzzle loaders from a time that was pre-Civil War, but could have been used in that war. Then there were Colt's, and Remington's, and Winchester's from the 1870s and a few from the early 1900's. These looked to be real deal and appeared to be in pristine condition. If they were real, then some of these would be worth a small fortune. The only modern era guns I saw were a Remington 12 gauge shotgun and a Smith & Wesson .38 revolver that were approximately 1970's vintage. Old Clem was quite the collector, I thought to myself. Absent mindedly, I moved my hand down to and pat the .45 I had strapped to my hip. I then remembered that I had left it hanging on a hat peg in the bedroom I was using. I made a mental note to myself to strap it on in the morning, so that I would not forget it when we left.

I was turning to head down the hall that led to my room, when I froze in my tracks. The heavy drapes were closed in the room, just as they always were, but I saw what looked like a light play across the drapes from outside. It was just one narrow beam like a flashlight would make, but it was a light just the same, and it was moving from left to right across the front windows of the house. I dropped to my good knee, and crawled over to one of the front windows and waited for the light to appear again. When it had not appeared after a few minutes, I slowly parted the drapes and looked outside. I saw nothing but darkness. I sat there for another few minutes, straining my eyes to see, and when nothing else happened, I got up and went to the door. It was bolted with a deadbolt that slid noiselessly open when I unlatched it. I slowly opened the door, stepped out onto the front porch and stood quietly listening and looking for any movement. It was warm but quiet. Must have been a reflection of car lights passing on the road, I thought to myself, even though I knew that we had not seen or heard a car pass since we arrived. After a few minutes, I went back inside, bolted the door, and went to bed.

I slept restlessly that night. I would close my eyes and wake up to what I thought were alternating points of light and darker shadows moving over my eye lids. I would open my eyes and the room would be dark, except for the light from the bathroom down the hall spilling under the door, onto the floor of my bedroom. I even got up out of bed a couple of times to part the drapes in my room and look outside, and to open the bedroom door and look down the hall. Of course there was nothing to see. This went on for a little while and then eventually stopped. I need to watch how much coffee I drink after supper; and what a stupid thing to dream about, I thought, as I drifted off to sleep again.

I sensed a presence standing over my bed and I awoke with a start to see Daisy's concerned but smiling face hovering over me, almost as if it were floating. "Hey sleepy head," she said.

"Geez Daisy, you really need to work on your bedside manner," I quipped. "You gave me quite a start there. What time is it anyway?"

"I came in here because I thought I should check on you. You sure were in a deep sleep. I have been trying to wake you for the last couple of minutes. I just wanted to let you know that breakfast will be ready in about 15 minutes and I did not want you to sleep through it. It is 8:15. We all agreed to have breakfast at 8:30, remember? Clem has been awake for a while and is already on his second cup of coffee. I brought one to you," she said as she motioned towards the night stand."

"Yes, I remember, and thanks. I will be out in just a few minutes."

I joined them, just as Daisy was setting out the pancakes on the table. "Good morning, Doc," Clem said with his usual morning cheer which had also been bolstered by two cups of caffeine.

"Morning, Clem," I acknowledged as I sat down.

The conversation that morning was nothing memorable. My head was feeling a bit cloudy and I was still thinking about the lights I saw, or thought I saw. Daisy asked a few questions about specifics from the story from last night, which Clem answered. Then she asked if there were any chores Clem wanted our help with, which there were not. He did repeat that he did have one more favor to ask of us, but he was not ready for it yet. No one mentioned seeing any lights or anything else unusual during the night, so I did not bring up my experiences. I wrote it off as too much late night coffee and too much family history, or a dream, or a combination of all three.

Since Daisy was up early to cook breakfast, I figured I could do my part. So, after everyone had finished eating, I washed the breakfast dishes while she went to shower. As I was finishing up, Clem walked in the kitchen and asked me to join him on the back porch. We stood there for several minutes surveying with our eyes the wreckage that had once been a very profitable farm operation and a wonderful backyard.

Pointing towards the graveyard that we had cleaned earlier, Clem said, "I know I told you and Daisy that my leg is buried in the grave next to Anne, and that the rest of my body is supposed to be buried there too one day."

"That's right. That is what you said," I responded.

"Well, I have changed my mind," he said looking down at his shoeless foot. "I don't want to be buried here after all. There are too many bad memories and I don't think Anne would mind. My leg is next to her, and I think that as long as part of me remains here, that she would like that. When the time comes, I have decided that I would like to be buried out there." He then pointed vaguely out in the distance.

I was not really sure what he meant, so I asked, "You want to be buried out in the field?"

"No, I mean I want to be buried out there." Again, he pointed out to nowhere in particular. "I want to be buried out in the desert in some unmarked and unknown grave. Kind of like the grave August has in the Mississippi River."

He then walked back inside leaving me on the porch wondering what the hell that was all about. After a few minutes, I walked back inside. Clem was already in the family room in his chair. "Would you mind making some more coffee, Doc?" he asked. "Then, when Daisy finishes her shower she can join us and we can finish this story."

"Be glad to, Clem," I responded. "You just sit here and relax. I know where everything is now and I will bring it all out when the coffee is ready."

Daisy joined us about 30 minutes later, and claimed her usual spot on the couch. Once we all settled in and had fresh coffee, Clem began the end of his family story.

"Roland's servant in St. Louis had followed through in his duties and all preparations for a repeat of the first trip further west were complete. He had done this in addition to making investments on Roland's behalf that made both men extremely wealthy. I have already mentioned these investments to you in several different places during this story, and there is no reason to go over them again. Suffice to say, that several generations of Roland's descendants, including the representative that you have spent the last few days with, were well provided for."

"Roland and Phillip were scheduled to leave St. Louis on a steamboat headed upriver to the Missouri River, and from there, take the Missouri to the jumping off point for the Santa Fe Trail. That steamboat was scheduled to leave in 3 days. The problem was that Roland no longer wanted to go. He had planned this trip to take his 3 sons out west and let them experience first-hand what he had experienced; but now, one of those sons was dead and one other had decided to remain on the Mississippi as a Captain's apprentice. Roland still had

Phillip to take along, but Roland's heart was no longer in it. Naturally, Phillip was concerned about his father and did not want to continue on without him. So, for the moment the whole expedition hung in the balance. The trip could always be postponed and a later steamboat could be taken, but for now, the entire remaining trip was in danger of being cancelled altogether. The men finally decided to make no decision that day. Roland and Phillip instead checked into the hotel that Roland's servant Ethan had reserved for them. Then, these two, plus the servant, met Captain Mayweather and Clement for dinner. The Captain was well known in the city and had several close friends with whom he had standing invitations to dinner whenever he was in town, as long as his wife was not with him. Captain Mike Mayweather's wife, Linda, was born and raised in Boston. He had brought her south, but she never liked the southern people. She found them to be backwards and slow talking. So, needless to say, she did not assimilate well. Over the years, as slavery became more and more of an issue, she adopted strong abolitionist sentiments and was quite outspoken about her beliefs. That pretty much sealed the deal and she was shunned by everyone south of the Mason-Dixon. However, the Captain was alone on this trip and he had contacted one of those friends and explained the situation regarding Roland and his sons. These friends welcomed the Captain and his new found friends, over for an evening of food and drinks."

"The next morning, Roland and Phillip met over breakfast to decide what to do. Roland stated to Phillip that he was not going any further on this trip. The trip no longer appealed to him, and he was going to stay in St. Louis for a month or so and become completely familiar with all of the investments and purchases his servant had made on his behalf. Then, once he was comfortable that everything was in order, and that he had a firm understanding of what he owned and the potential risks and rewards of each, he would return to England. Roland also stated that as much as he hoped Phillip would continue and go on without him, he was not going to force him to go. He left the choice entirely up to Phillip."

"Roland ended up staying in St. Louis for 3 months and then returned to New Orleans, where he stayed another month. He instructed Ethan to hold onto all investments for another 2 or 3 years. At the end of that time, Ethan was instructed to sell all of the holdings in cotton warehouses and steamboats, but to keep the land holdings and the railroad investments. Roland returned to England at the end of 1852 and never returned to America. He died in 1870."

"Phillip, my great grandfather as you know, spent the rest of the day weighing the pros and cons of whether to continue the trip, or cancel it and remain with Roland. That night, at dinner, he informed Roland of his decision to continue with the trip. Roland was delighted. Phillip did not have the same 'wild west' experience that his father had 6 years prior, but he did have his share of remarkable accomplishments. Phillip took the steamboat upriver to the Missouri River and from there to the jumping off station for the Santa Fe Trail. At this point, the guide who had been hired took over, and he led Phillip and his small wagon train down the Santa Fe Trail to New Mexico. Phillip briefly wrote of crossing through Comancheria, the territory of the Comanche's, and how this tribe of Indians demanded compensation for allowing passage through their territory. The Comanches were the most feared of all the Plains Indians. They were feared, not only because of their "no quarter" warrior culture, but also because they were one of the only two tribes that rode to a battle on horseback and then fought the battle on horseback. All other tribes dismounted, and then fought on foot. Fighting on horseback was something that the US Cavalry had not mastered, yet the Comanche had been perfecting this way of fighting for over a century. An interesting fact is that it was mainly due to the Comanche that Spain's, and then Mexico's, desire to push north and west did not progress any further. Another interesting fact is that during the Civil War, in 1863 to be exact, the Comanches actually closed down the Santa Fe Trail and no white men travelled it. This happened while the Army's attention was focused on fighting the Confederacy in the east.

After confirming with the guide that this demand for compensation was common, and also in their best interest to pay, Phillip paid the fee. He was lucky that he and everyone with him were not killed and scalped on the spot. After spending some time in New Mexico exploring, he decided to change the itinerary his father had laid out. The original trip was to turn east from New Mexico and head back to New Orleans through Texas, and then sail back to England. Instead, Phillip continued on to California and to the Pacific Ocean. Phillip stayed in America and only returned to England three times. The first trip was after the death of his mother in 1866. The second trip was after the death of his father in 1870, and the last trip was after the death of his oldest and only remaining brother in 1884. On this last trip he settled the family estate in England and sold to his nephews all of his inherited property and rights to property in England."

"Phillip married a Mexican girl in California, in 1858, and they lived and travelled around California, Mexico, and Arizona for the next 35 years. Hidali bore him 4 children. Three of them were girls. One was still born, and neither of the other two lived to see their 18th birthday. There was also one son, who would one day grow up, get married, have children, and become my grandfather."

"Phillip wrote in one of his journals of meeting Kit Carson in the area of Taos, New Mexico in the late 1850s, but there is no proof of that. He remained neutral during the American Civil War, even though his youngest brother was ferrying Confederate soldiers and material up and down the Mississippi River, until he was killed during the siege of Vicksburg, in 1863. To any that asked, Phillip claimed that he was a British subject, and therefore, he had no opinion on the war, even though he did have a very strong opinion that he kept to himself. According to the records, Phillip died in 1893, but there is no record of where he is buried. Family legend says that he died, and is buried, down in Mexico on his wife's family's property. He acquired lands and mines in California and Arizona, which were passed along, and occasionally a land or a mine holding would be sold off by descendants. This property which I live on and which I have farmed for decades, was one of those parcels of land that remained in the family. It eventually came under my control when my father died, along with the mine where you encountered the bees."

Clem stopped here and said, "Well, Doc and Daisy that pretty much ends my family story. I know most of it, and maybe even all of it was of little interest to you, but I sure appreciate you letting an old man tell it."

Daisy spoke first, "Don't be ridiculous, Clem, it was a wonderful story and I thoroughly enjoyed hearing it, just as much as I have thoroughly enjoyed your hospitality and company these last 3 days. Your family history is like reading a chapter of American history; only better, because your story puts flesh and blood on what are usually just events that happened in the past. I think that having the story told by a direct ancestor of the people involved is a treat beyond words. It made me realize that everyone has a family, and everyone's family has a story. It will not be exactly like yours of course, but everyone's story will have tragic moments and magic moments. Family history is what makes us who we are and places us where we are today."

She paused, just long enough for me to jump in. "I think what Daisy is trying to say, is that your story is a perfect example of how past decisions and choices are responsible for present day circumstances, and that is something that all of us have in common."

She shot me the expected dirty look, but I ignored it and continued, "Clem, I think we told you sometime over the last few days that Daisy and I love history and exploring sites, and discovering old things and making them new; or at least trying to find the story behind the old things and making that story live again. That curiosity of searching and finding out the 'what used to be', and the love of discovery when it happens, is what brought us to you. If we had not been driving around and taken a left turn and gotten lost, and then found that old mine, then we would never have met you. I agree with Daisy when she says that getting to know you over these past few days has been an indescribable treat. Your kindness is something that we will never forget and never be able to repay."

Clem smiled and bowed his head slightly. "I agree that we are all a product of our past. There is really no escaping it, but that does not mean the past has a strangle lock on any of us. Good people unexpectedly do bad things and bad people unexpectedly do good things. Things like that cannot always be easily explained by simply looking at someone's past decisions. Anyway, we could discuss that philosophy forever and never come to a concrete agreement. I just wanted to add that I am not a religious man, so I have not been praying; but I have been hoping that someone like the two of you would come along and spend some time with me and want to hear what I have to say. It has been a long time since I have had company. I have mentioned that to you, several times. I have enjoyed having you here as my guests, and to tell the truth, I have come to think of you more as family than as guests. However, I do have just two or three more things that I would like to relate to you. One of them is the promise I made to Doc to tell how my comfortable past life came to this state that you see now. Then, I have one short personal story that I would tell. I only hope that you will still have the same fond feelings about me that you have now, after you hear these last few things, and then I have a favor to ask."

We both nodded and waited for Clem to start. Several minutes passed, and during that time, we watched Clem struggle with what he wanted to say.

"I may as well get on with it," Clem finally said. "It was alcohol that ruined my farm, ruined my life, took my leg, and killed my wife. In the late 1980's, I had over 5 million dollars in cash in the bank. Just to give you an idea of how much that would be worth today, after calculating in cumulative inflation, I think the amount would be a little over 10 million dollars. In addition, I had clear title to all land and houses and equipment. I was debt free and flush with cash, but that obviously did not last. As you know, the basic beverages now in the house are coffee and water. That is all I offered you when you arrived, and that is all that I have served you while you stayed. I even told you the reason that those are the only beverages I offer, is because of a promise I made to my wife before she died."

"I really do not even remember how or when the problems with alcohol started. My wife and I would entertain friends, and sometimes these friends would come to visit and spend days and weeks with us. I was working hard and the farm was prospering and life was good. Then somehow things just got out of control. My two or three drinks on a Friday night, and the occasional Saturday night, somehow turned into two or three drinks on both nights. Then it was five or six drinks on those two nights. Before I realized it, I was having that many drinks and getting drunk every night. I was still working hard and the farm was doing well, so I thought that there was no problem. I deserved to have a little fun after all. I see now that it was a false front that I was putting up, and the only person I was fooling was me."

When he said this about the false front, I was reminded of the impression I had when he first showed us his backyard, a day or two ago, and the marked difference between it and the front yard and interior of the house. It dawned on me that could still be considered a false front and I wondered if he was aware of this similarity, but this fleeting thought was quickly replaced by Clem's voice talking on.

"Our friends and our youngest son stopped coming over as frequently as they used to, and they would not stay as long when they did come. Then, my wife just got quiet. By that, I mean she went from being actively interested in the farm, and in what I was doing, to just going through the motions and pretending. She was pretending to be interested and pretending to be happy and pretending that everything was okay. Then, she started asking me to slow down on the booze and she would attempt to monitor my intake. I wanted to explain to her the pain I was feeling, but I was always too drunk and too defensive to make coherent sentences. The harder she tried to help me, the more irritated I would become and the more I would drink. It became a continuous downward spiral that I could not break out of. It was like I was trapped in a whirlpool, and going around and around, and slowly sinking deeper and deeper into a bottomless pit of quicksand. The difficult thing to admit now is that I recognized some of this, but I no longer cared and I was not willing to do what it would take to break the cycle. I went through all of the money I had in the bank. I have no idea how, but it just melted away. Most likely, from me making bad decisions that I don't remember because I was drunk. I started taking out mortgages on the land and house. Not big loans, but enough smaller ones that taken together added up to a large loan that I could not repay. I stopped taking care of the farm. I stopped paying the workers. I stopped paying the bills. I basically stopped living, and as things got worse, I simply stopped. I just wanted to drink until I forgot. No one came over or invited us out any longer. It was killing my wife and I did not care about that either."

"The end came one night when I was blind drunk. I went to the shed out back and started the tractor. I am sure I had a reason for wanting to do that, but I don't remember what it was. I do not even remember going out back or starting the tractor. Apparently, my wife saw me and ran out the back door in an attempt to stop me. I did not see her and I ran over her, killing her instantly. I do not remember this happening either, and to this day I do not remember it. However, that is what the sheriff and the coroner that investigated the incident said happened. After killing my wife, I simply drove out into the field behind the house and rolled the tractor over trying to cross a ditch. My leg was pinned underneath and I was trapped there for the rest of the night and until mid-afternoon of the next day. When I began to sober up I remember wondering where my wife was, and why had she not come looking for me. A county policeman, who was driving by, happened to see the tractor lying on its side in the field and stopped to investigate. He found me under it, and he radioed for help and for an ambulance. Then, he walked back to the house found my wife dead in the backyard. The coyotes had gotten to her and he had to shoot a couple of them in order to drive the rest off. I was taken to a hospital, where my leg was amputated. When I was finally allowed home, what was left of my wife had already been buried in the plot we had set aside out back. I had my leg buried next to her, and as I stood there one morning, several days later, looking at my wife's grave, I promised to her that I would stop drinking. I only wish I had stopped before I killed her and lost everything. She was a wonderful woman. Both of you would have liked her. She told me many times when we were young, that all she ever wanted to be in life was a good wife, a good mother, and a tolerable housekeeper. Then, she told me many times when we were older that now those were the only things that she knew how to do and it made her happy to do those things. I think she excelled in all of them. It was me that let her down. I should have been tried and hung for murder, but I was not. My family had built up years of respect and influence, at least locally. The whole thing was hushed up and reported as an unfortunate farm accident. I guess there were enough people around who remembered me for the man I once was and they felt sorry for me. Or maybe, they thought sending me back here to live alone with the memories would be the worst punishment that I could be given."

There was silence for a minute or so after Clem stopped talking. I broke the silence by saying "I don't know what to say, Clem. That is a very sad story and I am sorry it happened to you, but it does not change my opinion of you that I have formed over the past few days. We all make mistakes and bad choices, the differentiator is how you respond and recover from those bad mistakes and choices. To me, it appears that you have made amends to your past. Obviously, nothing can bring back what you have lost, and maybe the best that can be done is to make peace with the past and do what you can to ensure you do not repeat it. It seems to me, that you have done those things."

"I agree with Doc," Daisy chimed in. "There has been a lot of sadness in your family history, Clem. From what you have told us, it is obvious to me that you come from a line of very strong people. The way your ancestors dealt with the sadness in their lives, echoes in the way you dealt with the sadness in your life. Regardless of fault, the common theme is that when sadness strikes, you and your ancestors faced it, acknowledged the cause, grieved, and then moved on. Like Doc, I am also sorry that this happened to you. Also like Doc, what you just told us does not change my opinion about you one iota."

"You are both too kind," Clem responded. "And I appreciate your words and your support, but I did not tell you these things because I was looking for your support. I told them to you so that you would have a full and complete picture of the man I am. Your impressions of me over the past few days are what they are, but those impressions were formed from incomplete data. I wanted you both to know the full truth. Sometimes, I wonder how much different my life would have been if Roland had never come to America, or if he had not left a business minded servant behind in St. Louis after his first trip, of if Phillip had not made the decision to leave Roland behind in St. Louis and then go to California instead of returning to New Orleans. If none of those choices had been made, then it is very likely my life would have been quite different. I suppose it is even possible that I would never have been born, if those choices had not been made when they were made."

Clem continued before either of us could respond, so we just nodded our heads. "There is one last thing I wish to tell you and then I will be done. My wife had an older sister. She was made an invalid from a degenerative muscle disease that struck her late in life. She required constant monitoring and assistance from trained medical caregivers, and so, we placed her in a home near Phoenix. My wife and I would go visit her once a week and sit with her and read to her. Sometimes, my wife would fix her sister's hair and they would talk about whatever it is that sisters talk about. These were small things, but they were all we could do, so we did them. After Anne died, I never went back to visit her sister. Part of the reason is that I did not want to face her. Even though she was an invalid, her mind was still sharp and I was a coward. Another reason I never went back is because the place gave me the creeps. The home was a 6 story main building, with wings of 3 stories on each side. It was made of brick and about 200 people called it home. Another 250 people called it work. It was basically a retirement center that offered different levels of care. In other words, a person could go there to live and be in full health or some lesser degree of health, and they would live in a non-assisted status. Then, as they aged, and their health deteriorated, they would move up to one of the multiple levels of assisted status. Each person would progress on the status ladder until they reached the top level, which is death, of course. Then they would be replaced by a newer and younger resident, who would begin their journey at the bottom of the status ladder and begin their slow move up."

"Kind of like corporate America, except the top level of the status ladder would be the end of a career instead of the end of a life. I think it is an interesting parallel," I said.

"I suppose you could look at it that way," Clem said, with just enough sarcasm in his voice to let me know his opinion of my comment. Then he continued, "Anyway, like I said, going there gave me the creeps. The lobby was comfortable and efficient and is what you would expect to see in a building that was part hospital and part condominium. The furnishings and atmosphere were nice enough. There were pictures on the walls and tiles on the floors. A warm fire crackled in the hearth and high-backed comfortable looking chairs were placed carefully and invitingly around it. There were gift shops and restaurants and a bar. There was even a post office and an internet cafe. However, it was the people who worked there that gave away the building's real purpose. They were nice enough in a friendly and efficient and medical sort of way, but there was no real closeness and no real effort expended to really get to know the residents. Everyone who worked there knew that there was no point in trying to build a long term friendship with the residents. This is understandable of course, but it is creepy when you think about it. Plus, sometimes, when Anne was doing her sisters hair, I would leave the room and walk down to the café. It was always so quiet and still in the halls, and it was this way whether I would walk them in the morning, or the afternoon, or late at night. There were times when I felt like I was not walking alone. I never saw a ghost, but I could feel them there; dead residents walking the halls, and climbing the stairs, and riding the elevators. Sometimes, I could even feel them watching from the walls, as if they were trapped in them now that their rooms were inhabited by newer and living residents. One night, I was coming back from a late dinner to pick up Anne, and as I stepped off the elevator on the floor that her sister lived on, I swear I saw Death sitting in the corner. He looked at me and our eyes locked, but he did not move. His eyes were deep and dark and shined slightly with a light of knowledge that is as old as the ages. I felt neither menaced, nor threatened. The presence I saw was peaceful, patient, watchful, fascinating, frightful, and beautiful all at the same time. After a few minutes, he gave a slight nod to me and broke eye contact. I guess the old bastard knows that if you want to go fishing, then you need to go where the fish are, but it was not me that he was casting for that day. I never mentioned this to Anne or her sister, and this happened before I started drinking heavily so I was not drunk."

Clem paused for a second, and then added with a laugh, "Maybe it would have been better if I had been drinking, because then I probably would not remember it. I guess my point in telling you this story, is that I got the impression that none of us have anything to fear from Death. It was a creepy experience for sure, but the actual presence felt rather calming and natural."

"Is she still alive?" Daisy asked.

"Who?" Clem responded.

"Your wife's sister of course," Daisy said rolling her eyes.

"Oh no, she was older than both Anne and I combined. Well, not really, but she was up there. She died a few years after Anne. She was cremated, but I did not attend the service. I am not even sure on whose closet shelf her ashes now rest on."

Clem paused briefly and then said, "Well, that concludes the story that I wanted to tell of my family and of the way I came to be in the state I am in now. I only have one last favor to ask and then I will be done, and you will be free to stay for as long as you like or leave and get back home.

"Sure thing, Clem, we'll do whatever it is you need for us to do, just ask." Daisy said.

"Same here Clem, we will be happy to do whatever you want us to do."

"Thanks," said Clem. "I appreciate it. The favor I want is that I want you to kill me., And I want you to remember what I told you on the back porch, and that is that I do not want to be buried here. So, I guess I am really asking for two favors," he said with a slight smile."

"What the hell, Clem!!" exclaimed Daisy. "You're kidding, right?"

He sat there silently, just looking back and forth from me to Daisy.

I said, "No, he is not kidding." Then I continued, "That is ridiculous, Clem. We cannot kill you. Why would you even ask us to do such a thing?"

Clem stood up from his chair and walked the 10 feet or so over to the fireplace. He leaned against the mantle with one elbow and then continued, "Because I am tired of living here alone with these memories," he said. "That is why I have been hoping someone like the two of you would stop by. I wanted to be able to tell the story you heard, and lift some of the weight that has been on my soul since Anne's death. Your visit allowed me to accomplish both of those things. Besides, I am an old man and will probably die soon anyway, but I don't want to have some sort of accident or illness and lie here suffering for days or weeks. I don't want to die here and have my body go undiscovered for weeks or months. Like I said, no one ever comes over for a visit. It is possible that I could die here and never be discovered."

I looked at Daisy and she looked at me. I could tell that she was upset and on the verge of tears. "Do something," she said to me.

Like what, I thought to myself. Then I spoke, "I understand that, Clem, but we would be happy to come out and visit you on a regular basis. We could come weekly or bi-weekly, or whatever frequency would make you comfortable. That way you do not have to worry about having something go wrong and no one knowing. We can even stay for a weekend every now and then. You can make a list of chores and we can tackle them together. Both the front and back yards need attention and we can do those first. Hell, I will even get you a cell phone so that we can chat daily if you want. We can figure out something, but you can just forget about us killing you. That is not going to happen."

"I am sorry, Doc, but this favor is not negotiable. If you will not do it voluntarily, then I will have to make you do it."

"How are you going to do that, Clem?" I asked.

"Daisy said that you always wanted to be in a gun fight," he said as he unhooked the dual action Smith & Wesson .38 from its hanging place over the mantel. Holding it in his hand and bouncing it slightly, as if weighing it, he looked at me and said, "Yes, it is loaded. I used to be a pretty good shot with this and with all of the firearms you see here. I never really liked the dual action though. Sometimes, pulling the trigger would throw my aim off by an inch or so. I prefer single action guns or just using single action mode on this one."

"Put the gun down, please," I said. "This is not funny, Clem."

He then stopped bouncing the gun and held it steady. I watched as he cocked the hammer back with his thumb and then, as if I was in a dream, I watched as he turned the gun towards me, until it was pointed directly at me and I was looking right into the barrel. I pulled the .45 I had on my hip out of its holster. As I raised the gun to level, my thumb engaged the hammer and pulled it back to fully cocked, all in one fluid motion.

Clem fired and I felt the bullet scream past my ear, before my eyes registered what had just happened. His bullet hit the window behind me and I heard the glass shatter. Instinctively, I pulled the trigger on my gun and I watched as Clem's upper lip exploded in a red and white cloud of shattered teeth and blood. The bullet exited the back of his head staining the wall behind him with bone and brain before imbedding itself in the wall, just below the mantel. The impact knocked Clem off of his leg and he fell over sideways, sliding down the wall and slumping to rest in a pile on the floor. I watched as his life bled out in a steady stream of blood and brains.

My ears were ringing from the sound of the shots, and I could hear Daisy's unbroken screams in the background. I knew she was sitting close beside me, but her screams sounded distant and far away. I felt my knees buckle and I remember falling to the floor and hitting my head on something hard. Then there was darkness.

12

When I woke up, I was in a hospital room. A woman in white was standing by my side with her hand on my wrist. "Welcome back Mr. Hardin. I am just taking your pulse. We almost lost you there a few times," she says to me.

I stared at her. Nothing seemed to work in my brain or my body. "Where am I?" were the only words I finally managed to get my brain to form.

"Phoenix Memorial Hospital," she replied. "You have been here for 5 days, in a medically induced coma for most of that time. You are still heavily sedated so don't talk too much right now."

My head was aching and my mouth tasted like it had been stuffed with cotton and then pissed in. The room started to spin and that is the last thing I remember her saying. I suppose I fell back to sleep. The next time I woke up, the nurse was gone. She had been replaced by another young female, also in white. She was accompanied by two males dressed in white, who were taking notes.

"Good Morning, Mr. Hardin" she says. "My name is Dr. Carol Christmas, and these two men are my aides."

I stared at her, trying to get my brain to function and send a question to my mouth. Finally, I was able to rasp out, "What happened?"

"It is a long story and we will fill in with the details soon enough." She said. "But for now, you need to rest."

I looked around the room trying to get my eyes to focus. "Hospital?" I managed to ask.

"Yes, she said, but you are going to be fine now and so is your friend. So, try to relax and we will be back later to talk." With that, she nodded to one of her assistants. Over my head was a bottle hanging from a metal pole. The bottle had a tube attached to it and I could follow that tube with my eyes and see that it was attached to a needle that was stuck in my arm. The assistant opened a valve at the bottom of that bottle, and that is all I remember of that visit.

The doctor came back, sometime later, and I was awake as she walked in the door. I remembered her face and I remembered that she was a doctor, but I could not remember her name or if she had told me why I was in a hospital. She walked over to me and smiled. I watched her but did not speak. She checked the machines that were monitoring my condition and then she checked the clipboard hanging at the end of the bed. Then she shone a light into my eyes that reminded me of the light I saw reflecting off of the drapes in Clem's house sometime earlier. Only after she was satisfied with what she saw, did she speak.

"Do you know where you are?" she asked.

"A hospital," I replied.

"Correct. Phoenix Memorial in fact. "Do you remember what happened or why you are here?"

I tried to think and recall, but my head was swimming with random disconnected pictures of events instead of actual memories of things that happened that I could focus on and play back and relive. "No, not really," I finally said.

"That is ok," she said. It is normal not to remember specifics so soon after your body experiences trauma. Your memory will improve and the events of the past few days will come back. Sometimes, the memories come back slowly, like a slow trickle. Then, sometimes, they come back in a rush, like a flood. Everyone responds differently and each way of memory recall is normal, so don't be upset if your memory is slow coming back or if it is quick."

"Can you get me started and give me some sort of refresher?" I asked.

"Yes," she said. You and your companion, Daisy, were attacked by bees about a week ago. You were stung over 1000 times and your friend was stung over 300 times. She would have been stung more but you covered her with your body which helped to protect her. You both were in critical condition when you were brought here. You almost died. In fact, you would both be dead if you had not been found by an older man, who just happened to see your jeep parked near his land and he went to investigate. He found both of your bodies lying near an old abandoned mine, where the bees had attacked. He said that the bees had built the biggest hive he had ever encountered in the mine, and the two of you had come too close and the bees attacked."

"Both of you were in a severe state of shock when you arrived, and while your friend was badly hurt, you were more so. You were unconscious when the ambulance brought you here, but you were convulsing and we had to restrain you. The ambulance attendants performed CPR on you on the way to the hospital and you flat lined once on the way here. They revived you while still in transport. When you arrived, your body was swollen and continuing to swell from the bee venom. In addition your respiration was so far off the charts that we had to do something to slow down both the swelling and the respiration. Before we could start, you flat lined again. We revived you a second time, but we were quickly losing you and knew that if you flat lined again, we would lose you for good. So, we induced a comatose state and packed your body in ice. You have been in a medically induced coma for the past several days. Once we had you stabilized, we could then focus on treating the stings and trying to save your life."

None of this made sense to me, except when she said the name Daisy. So I focused on that and did not really hear the rest of what she said. "Where is Daisy?" I asked.

"She was in critical condition as well, but she had less than half as many stings as you did. You actually saved her life by falling on top of her and covering her body with yours. She was still very sick when she arrived, but she recovered quickly. She is outside in the waiting area. She was released 2 days

162

ago, but she comes here every day and sits out in the waiting area. Sometimes, she is allowed back here and she will sit next to you and talk to you until we send her home. I will go tell her now that you are awake and that she can come in, but just for a few minutes. You still need to rest."

I was released from the hospital two days later, and over the next several days, I made marked improvement. Daisy was by my side constantly. We talked and the events slowly came back to me. I understood that the bee attack had almost killed us. I remembered that part and everything prior to it. However, when I would ask Daisy about Clem or the days we spent at his house, or his family story, or the gun fight, or the two of us trying to bury a body in the desert, or any of those things, she would tell me that none of that happened. The doctors confirmed that those memories were not real, but they were really not a dream either. The medical team explained that what I experienced was the brain's way of recovering and rebooting itself after such a life threatening trauma. Those events that I remember, while being real to me were, according to the doctors, basically nothing more than hallucinations brought on my trauma and drugs. I had my own different opinion of the events that I had experienced. I thought that I had experienced a vision of the family that had last lived on this land, but I only shared my opinion with Daisy.

Eventually, I asked the question that had been on my mind, but that I had been afraid to ask. I asked Daisy if she had met the man who found us and saved our lives. She responded that she had spoken to him but had not met him. She had asked the hospital about him after she was released. She told the hospital that she wanted to thank him. So, the hospital contacted him and he gave them permission to give Daisy his name and number, but Daisy had only spoken to him by phone. His name was Wyatt Peterson, and I asked Daisy if she would call him and arrange for us to meet him personally. I wanted to thank him too. Plus, I wanted to ask a few questions.

We met Wyatt 3 days later at a coffee shop in Wickenburg. After the introductions and thanking him for saving our lives, I asked him did he mind answering a few questions about the property he owned, and how he came to have possession of it, etc.

"Sure. But why do you want to know?" he said, eyeing me curiously.

"It is a hobby of mine," I said. "I work in the insurance business as an actuary, but I have always been interested in history and the stories of how things evolve."

"No offense meant, but that sounds like a boring hobby. Go ahead and ask your questions," he said.

"None taken and I have heard that before," I said with a smile. "When did you buy the land and what do you know about it?" I asked.

"I purchased the land at an auction" he said. "I really do not know that much about it because I am a farmer, and the reason I bought it is because of its farming potential. I am not all that interested in its history, but I will tell you the little that I do know about it. It was 8 years ago when I bought it. The land where the mine is located was bundled with another parcel of land a few miles down the road and both were to be sold together. The mine and the land it is on are pretty much worthless, but that parcel was a package deal with the other parcel, which is prime farming land. There was a large farm house on that property at one time, but it was foreclosed and seized due to non-payment of loans and back taxes. The foreclosure happened years ago, early to mid-nineties I think. Although it was, at one time, part of a family estate, no one was living there and the house was in really bad shape. The bank that took possession of the property had the house torn down because it had been vandalized beyond repair and it was a hazard. There was also what remained of a swimming pool in the backyard and the bank had it filled in for the same reason, and there were many mature palm trees on the property that were in the same area as the house. In fact the trees started at the road and led to the house, completely encircling it. The bank removed them as well. I understand that most of them were dead anyway. If you went there now, you would not be able to tell that a house once stood there. All that remains is a large field planted in 2000 acres of the prettiest corn you have ever seen. The only reason I was out at the property that day, was because of a small problem with the irrigation system. I was checking on the status of the repairs to that when I drove out to the mine on a whim. I was not even going to stop, but when I saw your jeep parked by the side of the road, I decided to stop and investigate. I was thinking that some kids were out there and playing around that old mine is dangerous, as you know."

"Do you know if there was a cemetery or a small family graveyard on the property? It would have been very small, with only a grave or two enclosed in a wrought iron fence."

"Yes, there is a burial on the grounds. There is no headstone and no fence, these were probably vandalized and stolen as well. The property records say a woman is buried on the grounds along with a possible second burial in the same area. The plots are out in the field and are marked so that no one plows them up. I do not remember the woman's name but you could look it up down at the courthouse if you want to."

"What do you mean by a possible second burial?" I asked.

"I am not sure what that means," he replied. "I remember this, because I thought it was odd. The records say there is a burial on the property and I remember it was a woman but I cannot remember the name, like I said. Then the records also say that there is another possible partial burial on the property but no other information is given on that as far as I remember. I suppose you could research that further if you wished too as well."

"So, you're not sure if there is an actual body buried there other than the woman's?"

"Correct. The partial burial could be the remains of someone killed in a war or in an accident where only pieces of a body could be recovered. Or it could be a memorial marker to someone who died and was buried elsewhere but the family wanted a memorial marker placed at home. Or, I suppose, it could even be a grave that was marked and recorded, but the person who it was intended for later decided to be buried somewhere else. Things like that happen. I suppose all of any of those are possibilities, but again, you could research it further if you want to."

"Yes, I agree. Things like that do happen," I said. "Thank you again for finding us and calling for help. We owe you our lives. We can never repay you, so please do not hesitate to ask if there is ever anything we can do for you. And thank you for taking the time to speak with me today. You have been very helpful."

We shook hands and Wyatt left. Daisy and I remained at our table and ordered another cup of coffee and a slice of blueberry pie. I was quiet, and she reached over and put her hand on mine but she did not speak. She simply left me alone with my thoughts.

After a few minutes, I stroked her hand and met her eyes. "Does what he said make you feel better?" she asked.

I had told her the entire story so she knew as well as I did that the part about the house and the pool and the cemetery matched up to what I had experienced in my hallucination, or vision, or whatever you want to call it.

"Yes, it does," I replied. "After hearing what Wyatt had to say, makes me want to drive out there and see if we can find where the house used to stand." I paused for a second or two and then added, "I just cannot shake the feeling that my vision included a message that Clem was trying to communicate to me, while I was unconscious. After all, the episode began when we trespassed on the property that his family used to own."

"Ok, I understand how you would feel that way. I am curious, what would you do if we find where the house once stood?" she asked.

"Then I would look for the cemetery, and when I find it, I will dig it up and see if there is a grave with a body and a grave with just a leg of course," I replied with a wink. "Who knows, maybe we will find a clue as well; but if there is no clue, and if all we find are the graves and if all we can determine is that one holds a body and one holds a leg, then we have a real mystery to work on. If that happens, then I will know for sure that my vision was real and there is a message that Clem wants us to find."

She laughed and squeezed my hand. Then looking up at me she said, "Well Doc, be sure to invite me along when you go," she said.

"Will do," I replied. I took a bite of pie and a sip of coffee. Then, looking at her, I asked, "By the way, do you still have that yellow sun dress you were wearing the day we left on vacation, prior to the bee attack"?

"Yes, why?" she replied.

I paused for a second or two and then responded, "Well, how about we go home and you change into it so that I can take it off of you?"

She blushed slightly and then replied, "You are always the hopeless romantic aren't you Doc?"

"Yes, I am," I replied with a grin. "It is both a gift and a curse."

"And completely charming and irresistible," she said, as she rose from the table and took my hand.